HER SECOND CHANCE COWBOY

BROTHERS OF MILLER RANCH BOOK ONE

NATALIE DEAN

D1522853

KENZO PUBLISHING

DEDICATION

I'd like to dedicate this book to YOU! The readers of my books. Without your interest in reading these heartwarming stories of love, I wouldn't have made it this far. So thank you so much for taking the time to read any and hopefully all of my books.

And I can't leave out my wonderful mother, son, sister, and Auntie. I love you all, and thank you for helping me make this happen.

Most of all, I thank God for blessing me on this endeavor.

EXCLUSIVE BOOKS BY NATALIE DEAN

GET THREE FREE BOOKS when you join my Sweet Romance Newsletter :)

Get One Free Contemporary Western Romance:
The New Cowboy at Miller Ranch - He's a rich Texas rancher. She's just a tomboy ranch employee. Can she make him see life can still be happy without all that money?

AND Two Free Historical Western Romances:
Spring Rose - A feel good historical western mail-order groom novelette about a broken widow finding love and faith.

Fools Rush In- A historical western mail-order bride novelette based off a true story!

Go to nataliedeanauthor.com to find out how to join!

CONTENTS

1

Chastity

*D*ark eyes stared out of the Amtrak train window, watching as flat plains whipped by. Forever unchanging, much like the town she was returning to.

Chastity sighed and rubbed at her temples. She always knew that she had to return home eventually, to visit, but she never imagined it would be because her father had died.

Ouch. The words were still so strange. Sure, her relationship with her father had never been excellent, and there was a lot of damage they needed to talk about, but now she supposed the opportunity for that was gone. Because he was gone.

Chastity closed her eyes, trying not to remember the call that she had received from her mother, the usually stoic woman crying so hard she was barely intelligible. Her mother and father had been together for so long. His death was like someone had stolen the sun from her world.

For the smallest of moments, she had debated telling her mother she couldn't come. After all, she was a month behind on all her bills and hadn't landed a single gig in months. Although it made her stomach twist with shame, perhaps a month or so with her mom would help her catch up on her bills. It wasn't like she was giving up, just rallying before trying again.

But as she watched the plains rush by, that resolution was beginning to fade. While she had never been that close with her parents—mostly due to their *very* specific ideas on what a woman should or shouldn't do with her life; and running away to the big city without a husband was definitely not on their list —she had an even colder relationship with the town itself.

She had been picked on plenty enough in her younger years to know that the town she grew up in wasn't kind to dreamers. She didn't know what got her more derision, her plan to go off to college in New York City and make a living for herself, or her desire to be an actress. If she had a dollar for every time someone told her that she couldn't make a living as an actress... well, she could have made a living off it.

And now she was going back, tail tucked between her legs in failure.

No, she had to remind herself. This is just a temporary setback. You'll keep at it once you're on your feet again.

Chastity looked down at her old, battered phone in her hand, where she still had her gallery open to the obituary she had helped her mother write. While she did have a lot of bad feelings and memories tied to the town, there were a lot of wonderful, warm ones too.

Living in New York City had been... eye opening, that was for sure. Often times it seemed that the walls of stone were made of ice, as were the hearts of those around her. Everyone was so cold, so unfeeling, and they rarely warmed enough to let someone into their pre-formed circles.

The friends she had when she was younger were the kind of friends some people would kill for. Despite not wanting to return to her hometown, she found herself looking forward to seeing them again. Reconnecting with old friends so she didn't have to feel so isolated in a city full of people who were struggling to get by, just like she was.

"Could I get you a drink?"

Chastity looked over her shoulder to see one of the train attendants with a cart. Smiling, she requested a bottle of water, and he slid it into her hand, free of charge. She didn't know if it was complimentary for all the passengers, if he was giving her special treatment because he'd peeked at the morbid paperwork in her lap, or if this was some sort of strange way of hitting on her. But no matter the reason, she drank it down gratefully.

"How long until we're to our destination? Soon, right?"

"Ma'am, this is a cross-country line, so our final destination won't be for over a day. What stop are you specifically looking for?"

"Oh. Blackfish County?" She didn't know why she said that with such hesitation. She had grown up there her entire young life.

"That's about four more hours away. Why? Are you anxious to be back home?"

"Yeah... something like that."

"Try to hold your horses, if you can. We'll be there soon enough, I promise."

He gave her a strange wink, which she also wasn't sure how to take, and then he continued to push his cart along.

Goodness, being in the big city had certainly damaged her

ability to tell who had ulterior motives and who was just being nice. Hopefully her time in town would have a positive effect.

That was unlikely, however. Her relationship with her parents had always been... tenuous, to put it nicely. Ever since she was young, she had this feeling of never being good enough for them. She loved theater and started performing in school plays; her father tried to force her to stop and take home economics classes instead. When she did it anyway behind his back, he said he didn't want her to be a starving artist and a bum.

She wished it stopped there. While she believed in equality, he was several generations behind. He thought her ultimate goal should be to find fulfillment as a stay-at-home mom, who never left the confines of their small town. And he had no problem telling her what he thought every time she visited. It was like he was gloating that her career hadn't taken off.

So, eventually, she had stopped visiting altogether. Seeing his smirk as he asked what plays or shows she had landed since he last saw her was far too grating, and her mother often echoed his sentiments.

Her situation was difficult, because she did love them, but she didn't love how they made her feel. In fact, she *hated* how they made her feel, and *that* was most likely why she had been avoiding them for the past few years.

There was, she knew, another person she had been avoiding. And, hopefully, she wouldn't accidentally run into *him*.

Chastity shook her head, dismissing the thought and anything related to it. *Focus girl. You're in town to help Mother with Father's funeral and make sure that she is set up to survive without him.* She would offer emotional support, and that was it. She was going to visit like it was a small vacation, and then pick up her bags and run away before the small town could suck her back in again.

After all, it had taken her seventeen years to escape the bonds that held her there, and just because she was back for a short while didn't mean that it was time to repair those broken links. Some things needed to stay in the past, where they could be viewed with nostalgia-tinted glasses.

"It's just temporary," she reminded herself, looking out the window once more.

At twenty-eight years old, her future seemed as empty and barren as the fields they were passing. She needed some direction, something to tell her that she wasn't crazy for wanting to live outside of the wife-box that her hometown had been so eager to throw her into. She needed... *something*, but she didn't have words for it.

But whatever it was she was seeking, she doubted she would find it in Blackfish County.

2

Chastity

*T*he train pulled to a stop, surprisingly quiet and without a jolt. Chastity grinned at her own naivete. What did she expect? Some sort of old-timey coal engine, whose tires screeched and whistle blared for miles? Not unless she had been suddenly thrust back into time.

Chuckling to herself, she stood and pulled her bags from an overhead bin. She had lived in town long enough to know that the train station had once ended at a bustling city about an hour's drive from home. But over the years, they had laid more and more tracks until it finally reached the heart of their sleepy little town of Blanche Creek.

Their economy centered around the ranches, naturally. And the ranchers were an independent lot who valued tradition. Generations of families, one right after another, were born and died on their ranch. Never getting out to see the world.

Chastity shook her head at the thought. As far as she was concerned, her presence wouldn't go beyond the town border, so she didn't need to think about the ranches. They could stay tucked into the background noise of her life where they belonged.

Looking out the window made Chastity feel a bit washed up. Here she was, back at the same train station she'd left right after high school, when she'd been full of dreams. But she had absolutely nothing to show for all of her years of work since she graduated.

It took quite a bit of willpower to raise her chin as she descended the steps off the train. She'd had a few hiccups in her plan. But she wasn't out for the count yet. She would persevere. Maybe she'd get a callback for the latest show she'd auditioned for—

"Chastity?"

The warble of a familiar voice brought her out of her introspection, and she saw none other than her mother standing there, tear streaks down her face and a tremor to her mouth. Naturally Chastity's heart melted right then and there. Dropping her bags, she ran and threw her arms around her mom in a hug.

Her mother leaned against her heavily, her face tucking into where Chastity's shoulder met her neck. Chastity could already feel tears trickling down to wet the collar of her shirt, and for once, she was at an utter loss of what to say.

"I'm sorry," Chastity whispered, gently rubbing her mother's back. "But I'm here now, okay?"

"Yes," her mom said, her voice still shaking. "You're back home. You're here."

"Yes, I am, temporarily." Chastity fished into her purse and brought out a packet of tissues she had shoved in there, figuring that she would need them, considering the reason for her trip. "How about we go home and settle in?"

Her mother nodded and finally pulled away, taking the tissue to wipe at her damp face. After a few more tender seconds, where Chastity gently gripped her arms, she took several deep breaths to collect herself.

Chastity took a moment to examine her mother. Three years had passed since either of them had visited each other for the holidays, and she could see the years worn into her mother's face. Her crow's-feet had grown deeper while the lines around her mouth had dragged down farther by the relentless hand of gravity. There was a slight cloudiness to one of her eyes, and she stood a bit crookedly, as if one of her hips was hurting her.

It was quite different from the gray-haired yet spry woman that she had seen three Christmases ago. What all had she missed?

Too much, she told herself as her fingers interlaced through her mother's. But she was home now, and she was going to fix that. Even if it was only long enough to get her mom back onto her feet and through the grieving process, Chastity would make sure she didn't have to go through this alone.

Goodness knows, Chastity was aware of how soul-sucking loneliness could be from her time spent in the city. The isolation was like a gaping maw, always eating at both time and happiness until nothing was good and everything was daunting.

"You ready?" she asked gently, giving her mother another soft hug.

"Quite," her mom answered, composing herself into a bright smile. "We might even catch the ice cream cart rolling by."

"Goodness," Chastity said with a laugh. "Is Flannigan still at it?"

"It's his son, actually. Marty Junior."

Chastity felt a strange sort of twist in her stomach that she couldn't quite name. "Oh, he just stepped right into his dad's footsteps?"

"Yes. Started right after high school with them together, and after Flannigan had that stroke, he took over the whole thing." She sighed and pressed her hand against her heart. "They're such a lovely family. They offered for me to come stay with them, but I turned them down when you said you were going to come back home for a bit."

"Wow, that was nice of them." There it was. That small-town hospitality and looking out for each other that she had missed.

"It really was. But even staying in their fancy place couldn't compare to having my little girl back in town. Oh! We have so much to catch up on. Your father's—" she stopped short, and Chastity halted as well, feeling her mother's grip tighten on her arm. "Oh dear. I'd forgotten."

"It's okay, Mom," Chastity murmured, wrapping her arm even more firmly around her mother's slim figure. Had she lost weight? Chastity wasn't sure she liked that.

"I—I would very much like to go home now."

"Of course. Let's keep walking."

Thankfully, the town was small enough that it was only about a ten-minute walk home, and the temperature was mild. As they walked, multiple people tipped their heads or offered their condolences, and Chastity recognized almost all of them.

In fact, it seemed like nothing had really changed in the small town. Storefront after storefront, the post office, the town hall. All of it was the same colors, the same structures. Even the video rental store that had caused such a ruckus when it moved into town when she was a wee little girl had survived. Funny how that stood the test of time when almost all the other shops had been handed down for generations since the founding of Blackfish County.

Even though it was only a ten-minute walk, the last part seemed to take forever, as all the history of her life in the town began to weigh down on Chastity's mind like a ball and chain. When they finally did walk into the unlocked front door of her mother's house, she felt a weight lift from her shoulders.

"Would you like some tea?" Mother asked, smiling sweetly to her daughter.

Chastity nodded before pressing a kiss to her mother's cheek. "I would, thank you."

"Perfect. Why don't you go up and get your things squared away while I get the kettle going?"

"Sounds good."

Chastity headed up the stairs, and as she did, it felt like she was going back in time. The wallpaper was the same. The photos were the same. Even the vanilla and lemon smell of the house was the same.

She reached the door to her room and opened it carefully, remembering how it loved to swing open wildly and how many times her father had to patch the wall behind it. Sure enough, her room was exactly how she had left it the last time she had been around, three years earlier.

Letting out a long breath, Chastity let her stuff fall to the ground and looked all around, taking it in. Not a speck of dust anywhere, which meant that her mother had been cleaning her room this entire time, just in case she ever visited.

Or that she had gone into a cleaning frenzy after Chastity announced that she was coming home to help. But judging by the fact that it had only been three days since her father's passing and her mother's emotional reaction at the train station, she doubted her grieving mom would have had the time or energy to clean it after he died.

But that just made the guilt stab at Chastity that much harder. Why had she let so much time go by? Yeah, she hated the way her parents would constantly wheedle at her dreams, dismissing all the hard work she had done so far just because she didn't have any dollars to show for it. And yeah, her father would always pressure her about getting married while her mother would drop hints about wanting grandchildren.

But still... they loved her. They had never raised their hand against her, had never called her names. They told her how smart she was and how lucky they were that she was their daughter. They just... were products of their time, Chastity guessed.

Flopping back onto her bed, she let herself deflate for a minute. There was a whole lot of baggage to unpack, both literal and metaphorical, but with any luck, she could just shove it all into a closet until she left again.

3

Ben

*B*en looked over the empty part of the barn that he was rebuilding and expanding with his younger brother, Benjamin—Benji for short. Often people were confused by their similar names, thinking that Ben's nickname was short for Benjamin. But instead, the eldest of the current generation of Millers had the first name of Benedict, while his younger brother's nickname was Benji. Was it confusing? Yes. But his mother had wanted to give all of her sons names starting with B, just as the previous Millers all had names starting with M.

It was a peculiar tradition, and he had been quite shocked when he had learned that not every family named all their children with the same first consonant. It had seemed convenient to him at the time, but now he realized, it was a bit strange.

Oh well. The Miller family was rich, so they could afford a little bit of eccentricity.

"What'cha thinking?"

Ben looked down from the loft he was standing on to see Benji below him, a toolbelt slung over one of his shoulders. He had previously been doing all of the work on the renovation himself, so he was glad to see one of his younger brothers present, but there was something... *off* about the whole thing.

He couldn't quite put his finger on it, but lately he had felt a growing sort of dissatisfaction. Normally, his chores and projects around the ranch were plenty to keep him going, but lately it had seemed like there was something missing. Something intangible, maybe even inexpressible, but it sat right in his gut and left a sour sort of taste in his mouth.

"Nothing," he replied flatly. No need to clue his brother in and have them all worried. They had enough on their plates with everything else going on. Goodness knew there was never really downtime on the ranch. There was always something that needed fixing, planting, or replacing.

The cows were all frolicking out in the expansive meadows south of the ranch, being tended to by their cousins on the Ramsey side of the family, while Bart was back at the main house with mother. Ben would have liked to have him there, but he knew his next brother in line wasn't quite ready to get back to everyday life yet.

Not after...

"Hey, you done daydreaming up there or what?"

Ben shook his head and slid down the ladder, using a technique Pa had taught them all when they were young boys. It never failed to make him feel a bit like an action hero, but that good feeling fled when he took a step away from the bottom of the ladder only to put his foot down—right into an old cow pie.

"You have got to be kidding me," Ben murmured, wiping his boot on some long hay. Though it was certainly not unusual for ranch life to be full of poop and animal waste of all kinds, he normally wore his muckin' shoes for walking around in that. Since he was focusing on construction today, he'd worn his nice, steel-toed boots for protection. "That's gonna be a son of a gun to get out of the tracks."

"Yeah, it is," Benji said with a laugh. "You better not take those shoes onto any of Mama's rugs. I don't care if you're a grown man, she'll definitely skin ya for it."

"Ain't that the truth," Ben said with a laugh. Looking back up to the rafters, he clicked his tongue. "So, how do you wanna do this?"

"I'm not entirely sure," Benji admitted. "There's a couple of ways that I see, but I'm not sure of the math of it all. You want me to call Brad out here?"

Ben shook his head. "Nah, he's either breaking our new horses in or working with the preservation society on the reservation. We'll have to make do ourselves. Besides, it's not like you and I haven't done this before."

"I know, but geez, if he isn't some kind of genius with the whole process. I swear he can whip up a blueprint in the time it takes me to tie my shoes."

"He does have a knack for it," Ben admitted with a nod. As the second to youngest brother, Bradley had been the most bookish of all of them. While he could throw down with the rest of them, he still had an uncanny skill with a protractor and calculator.

"Too bad he doesn't have that same knack for all the beautiful women he's meeting down on the rez," Benji said with a snicker.

"Oh, like you're so much better?" Ben shot back, turning to his tool kit that he had trundled here from their main barn.

"Hey, you know that I *choose* to remain single because I got tired of all the gold diggers that flooded in once each of us turned eighteen. But Brad... I don't know if he even realizes that women exist."

"I'm sure he does," Ben said with a wry grin.

His brother wasn't kidding about those looking for money. The Miller Ranch had made a bit of a name for itself in the generations since it was founded. Built on love, respect, and kindness, the family made a motto of putting their money where their beliefs were and made sure everything out of them was one hundred percent.

Of course, as time passed, it became impossible to keep up with the inhumane demands of industrial farming. It was Ben's grandfather who faced the decision whether to keep his cows pregnant as much as possible, never letting them run or play, and constantly taking their calves away, or to fold up shop and live off the considerable wealth that the family had built up. It was then that Grandmother Miller had an idea, and the whole issue was turned upside down.

According to her, she could taste the sadness in the meat she ate or the milk she drank when she traveled, and she suggested that other people probably could too. And even those that couldn't probably would prefer that their meals were treated with the respect that humans were supposed to give animals as God's appointed shepherds. So, the Millers had kept their operation small, but began an advertising campaign about how the cows were allowed to play whenever they wanted, only got pregnant naturally by their own rhythm, and usually lived with their calves for most of their lives. Of course, there were still some people who thought any form of farming was cruel, but a massive chunk of animal lovers were thrilled to get meat from animals that weren't tortured, and suddenly the Miller fortune shot into the millions.

And where there were millions, there would always be people desperate to do anything for that money. And gold digger women.

"I dunno. Do *you* even realize that women exist? I swear, I've never even seen you look at a beautiful lady, and Lord knows plenty have tried to get you to turn your head to them."

"Why are you so obsessed with women all of a sudden?" Ben deflected, grabbing his checklist and going over to the pile of lumber he had brought in from outside of the barn. "You lonely?"

"Aw, come on, don't change the topic like that. If I didn't think it were crazy, I'd say you haven't really loved anyone since—"

"I'm done talking about this," Ben said quickly. "We have too much to do to waste daylight daydreaming about romance."

"All right, whatever you say, brother."

At least Benji knew when to let the subject go. Quietness descended, as Ben went over his blueprint again, making sure he had all the supplies and everything was aligned as it was supposed to be. Some might accuse him of being overly careful, but he preferred to think of it as being thorough. Measure twice, cut once? More like measure five times, double check again, then cut. That was his motto.

Just when he was about done with his overview and ready to get the first pieces of lumber out, there was a loud knock on the barn door. Turning, he saw his brother Bart standing there quietly.

"Hey, you got out of the house," Ben said, grinning at his next brother in line.

But the well-built man just nodded, continuing to stand there and looking over the barn like it was completely foreign to him.

"Are you all right? Are you having one of those, uh... those moments?"

He shook his head and seemed to come to his senses. Clearing his throat, he spoke, which was a rare thing nowadays. "Mama would like to talk to you."

"Right now? Is she all right?" Although Mrs. Miller was the epitome of good health, Ben couldn't help but feel a spike of alarm. The world could be a very cold and cruel place, so he was always wary of the worst happening.

But Bart was already walking off. Ben wasn't sure if he should be going anywhere alone with how he was acting, so he handed his tools off to Benji and trotted after him.

"It's some good weather we're having today," Ben said when he was still several steps behind his brother. He had learned the hard way to never surprise his brother by sneaking up behind him. The best thing to do was introduce your presence before you were within arm's reach.

"Yeah. It's nice."

"Maybe one of these days we can go for a ride. I know your little mare Juliette misses you."

"Does she?" He seemed to think on it a moment, but his eyes were somewhere far off. Somewhere none of the family could quite reach. "Yeah. That sounds like it would be nice. Like the old days."

"Yeah, exactly, like the old days. Before—" Ben cut himself off. There were certain words—triggers is what the doctors called them—that they weren't supposed to mention during Bart's recovery. "Things went sideways."

"Yeah. I'm gonna go fix up some lunch. You want something?" Ben shook his head no. "All right. Ma's in the sitting room, last I knew." And with that he wandered into the main house, heading to the kitchen to rustle up something from the fridge. Ma always kept it full of snacks and treats, so there was no doubt he would find something tasty.

While most of the brothers stayed in their own places that they'd built all across the Miller's spread of land, Ben and Bart stayed at the main house. Granted, Bart had his own place by one of the creeks, but given how much he was struggling with adapting to everyday civilian life, it'd been decided it would be best for him to live at the main house for a while in his old room.

But Ben... well, as the eldest he had never strayed far. While he had left his teenage bedroom right around the age of twenty, he had chosen to build his cozy bachelor's cabin right beside the main house with a long hallway to connect the two build-ings. It gave him enough privacy to be his own man but kept him close enough to the main house, so he could still keep his finger on the heartbeat of the Miller Ranch.

Plenty of people thought that being a rancher was relatively easy, especially one that had its own brand set up and had been around for generations. However, Ben had dedicated his entire life to training to one day take over, and he still learned some-thing new every day. Thirty years eating, sleeping, and breathing that Miller life, but he still had a long way to go.

"Ah, there you are," Ma said from the couch, her fingers flying as she knitted something. A blanket maybe, by the look of her yarn choices. "I was hoping you weren't too far out."

"Just working on the barn, Ma. You wanted to speak with me?"

"Ah yes, I have a favor to ask of you, but you are completely welcome to say no."

That piqued his interest. Normally, Ma was an all-or-nothing sort of woman. "What d'ya need?"

"Unfortunately, an old family friend of ours has passed and the wake is tomorrow. I was hoping you would go with me."

Ah. That was indeed unfortunate. It seemed his parents were getting to the age where their friends were either dead, dying, or had forgotten themselves. "Who was it, if you don't mind me asking?"

"You know him, actually. You were once quite close, which is why I want you to go with me."

Ben could sense when his mother was burying the lead and stood a little straighter. "Who passed, Ma?"

"Mr. Parker. Aneurism, sadly. It's quite tragic. I feel terribly for Ruby, so I thought I would bake her some nice things so she doesn't have to cook for a bit."

At the sound of the Parker name, Ben's blood rushed through his body, making his ears burn hot and his face color with bright red. He could feel the heat creeping across his cheeks, but he fought to tap it down along with all the memories that came along with it.

A happy smile and joyous laughter. Long black hair swishing in the wind, reflecting the summer sun. Soft lips pressed against his, hand squeezes and hugs.

The images grew on themselves, filling out like an artist slowly adding color to a picture until a scene that he had long since buried was playing before him.

"I don't understand why you have to do this."

"Because it's my dream. You remember what it's like to have a dream, right?"

"But dreams aren't real. I'm real. Please!"

"I'm sorry. I'm so, so, so sorry. But this is what I have to do."

Ben snapped himself out of the memory and forcefully

shoved it as far down as he could into the dredges of his psyche. When was the last time he had thought of that specter of his past?

Of course, his mother caught onto his expression. "I'm fairly certain only Ruby will be there. She doesn't really have anyone to support her now, considering her daughter lives in the Big Apple and hasn't come back in years."

"She's still in New York City?"

"As far as I know."

Ben felt a flicker of guilt. He had just heard that poor Mrs. Parker was a widow and suffering through the death of the love of her life and the first thing he had worried about was himself. That was awfully selfish, and Ben didn't like being selfish.

"Yeah, I'll go with you. I should pay my respects as it is."

"Thank you, dear. Let's hope that something good can come out of this tragedy and poor Ruby can reconnect with old friends."

"Yeah, let's hope."

4

Chastity

Chastity took a long drink of water from her cup before setting it on the table beside her. The wake had started barely ten minutes prior, and there was already a long line of people waiting to give their condolences. It was overwhelming, and she felt like she had been thrust into a grand ceremony without properly preparing herself.

Sure, she had known that she was coming down for her father's funeral. She had been going over the funeral home bill and ordering the death certificate and pretty much everything. But now, seeing his body in the casket, his pale, wrinkled face impassive... his death was suddenly very real.

And yet it wasn't.

That cold, unmoving face in the casket wasn't her dad's. He had always been an expressive person. She could remember the pink in his cheeks as he saw her report card, a wide grin soon following before he hung it on the fridge. She could remember the way his forehead furrowed when she told him she was cast as a lead in the school play, and she wasn't going to quit. She could remember him leaning over, red eyed and scared, as she burned with a fever that she caught during freshman year.

He had loved her, in his own way. Sure, that didn't erase the mean things he did, or give her closure to the way he derided her life, but he was dead. There wasn't much to do now but forgive him, she guessed.

Chastity just wasn't sure she was ready to do that yet.

How stressful! Her stomach was flip-flopping as people began to approach them, all somber and serious. But if she was feeling a bit stressed and teary-eyed over it, she couldn't imagine what her mother felt. Charles and Ruby Parker had been together for forty years. They had about given up on having children before Ruby got pregnant with Chastity. Although Chastity had her fights with them growing up, and different ideals, their love for each other had been apparent to anyone who saw the two together. Chastity remembered hoping when she was younger that she would someday find someone who looked at her how her father had looked at her mother, but so far that had yet to happen.

Well, there was one man who had gazed at her like that, but—

She cut *that* thought off fast. It was not the time to be thinking about old drama. She was here to help her mother and mourn the loss of her father. Although they had never really been close, she'd never wanted him to die. And now that he was gone, she couldn't help but wonder about all the ways he would be missed—and all the things she never got to say to him.

The first people came up, an older couple that Chastity didn't recognize. Maybe church friends? She had stopped going when she was sixteen, so most of the parishioners had faded from her memory.

However, Mom clearly knew them, because the two women tottered toward each other and linked together in a teary hug. The gentleman, dressed in what had to be his Sunday finest, offered his hand to Chastity.

"We're so sorry for your loss."

"Thank you," Chastity murmured, feeling the back of her throat squeeze. She had managed not to cry since arriving, but she didn't think her streak was going to make it through this crowd.

"Agatha was worried about you two having to cook with everything you've got to do, so we brought you a bit to eat."

It was only then that Chastity noticed he was holding a black, insulated bag in his other hand. The funeral home that they were renting had anticipated this, however, and Chastity found herself repeating the words they had told her.

"The door to the left over there leads to a table where you can set it down for us to collect when we go home. If it needs to be kept cold, there's a refrigerator too."

"Right. Of course. You let us know if you need anything, ya hear? Charles was a good man and helped a lot of people."

"We will. Thank you so much."

The older women finally parted, and the elderly gentleman moved on to my mother, kissing the top of her head before pulling her into a hug as well. That was another thing Chastity had missed about home, *touch*.

Walking around in New York City, it often seemed that everyone had a barrier around them that you weren't supposed to penetrate, and if someone did dare to touch another human being, they were usually up to no good. It was exhausting to always be on guard, to be closed off and defensive. But here, back in town, everyone was so much more *connected*. It made her wonder why she was so determined to go back to the city anyway. It made her miserable.

Because if you want to be an actress or entertainment talent, you have to be in either LA or NYC, and that one was the farthest from your parents.

Ouch. That thought hurt, but it was true. Goodness, having a tenuous relationship with her parents certainly complicated things.

But then the next couple was up, someone she recognized as her fifth-grade science teacher and her husband. Chastity remembered that her mother used to be involved in the school's PTA and drama club when she was younger, and that was how the two women had met.

"It's so good to see you!" the woman said, rushing forward for a quick hug. "I'm so terribly sorry it had to be under these circumstances though."

"I know what you mean," Chastity said wanly, pulling away to give her husband a firm handshake. But he too reached out to gently pat her arm, even though they really didn't know each other that well. Small town love was something else. "It's wonderful seeing everyone, but it'd be nice if it wasn't over something that makes us all cry."

"Exactly." She pointed to her husband's other hand, and Chastity saw that he was also carrying a bag. "I don't know about you, but when I'm stressed, I just get the worst sweet tooth, so I made you a couple of pies."

"Thank you so much." Chastity repeated the same set of directions that she had given the other couple, and the woman stood on tiptoe to give her a kiss on the cheek before going over to her mom.

And so, it went, person after person, couple after couple.

Mostly elderly folk, but plenty of younger people too. If Chastity didn't know better, she'd say nearly the entire town came out to wish them well.

That thought was overwhelming. All of these people were involved in her father's life, and she was off galivanting across the country. And by galivanting, she meant failing at her dream and wondering if she could afford the extra dollar to get the spaghetti sauce that she really liked instead of the generic brand.

And for what? So she wouldn't have to hear comments about how she should be having children already? Or that she needed to settle down and find a husband. Or that it was her job to submit to—

Okay, actually she had some pretty good reasons for leaving. So why did she feel so guilty about it?

She glanced to her mother to double check on her, and although her face was lined with tears, she seemed to be doing all right. Perhaps everyone's kindness was helping her get through things. Or perhaps she was just showing that patented Parker stubbornness and refusing to completely break down in front of others.

Chastity crossed to her, grabbing some extra tissues along the way and placed them in her hands. Leaning in, she rested her head on her mother's shoulder. "Do you need a break?"

"No, sweetie. I'm all right. There are a lot of people waiting still."

"There really are." Chastity straightened and returned back to her spot, squeezing another pump of hand sanitizer into her hand. Looking up, she saw who she recognized as the pastor of the town church.

But as he reached out his hand, a particular voice caught her attention. Somewhere between velvet and rumbling thunder, there was a timbre that tickled at the back of her mind, making her heart skip a beat.

Thoroughly distracted, Chastity looked past the man as he shook her hand, and she focused her gaze down the line. Just like the last ten minutes, there were faces she recognized, faces she didn't, and some that straddled the line between recognition and faded memory.

But not *him.*

Her heart stopped the moment she laid eyes on him. He was taller and brawny, having filled out with the muscle of manhood, but there was no mistaking him.

Towering over everyone else around him, his sandy-blond hair was cut close to his head on the sides and groomed long on top. Even from the distance she was at, Chastity could make out his piercing green eyes surrounded by dark, dark lashes. He was wearing the same Sunday best as everyone else, but his muscles were filling it out so much it was borderline indecent.

His jaw was as sharp as ever, able to slay a thousand Philistines or cut through steel, and his cheekbones were as high as she remembered. All in all, it was like God had personally sculpted him to absolute perfection.

Before she could catch herself, Chastity took a step forward. It didn't take long before those dazzling green eyes noticed her movement, and they landed right on her, staring through her like she was thinner than a sheet of paper.

Her breath caught in her throat, and it felt like her soul up and left her body. But while her mind was in shock, her mouth kept on moving right along without her brain.

"Benny?"

5

Ben

"*B*enny?"

Dear Lord, her voice was as enrapturing as he remembered, and he had to close his eyes not to get caught up in it. Ben couldn't believe that *she* was here. Wasn't she supposed to be in the city?

Her voice was low for a woman, with a very specific laugh that was just on the border of being salacious or unpleasant. But undercutting those potentially off-putting traits was an alto-tone that was smoother than honey, making each of her words hang in the air like forbidden fruit.

Dozens of feelings hit Ben at once. Revulsion, desire, heartbreak, shock. It was a kaleidoscope of thoughts and emotions that left him breathless.

"Are you all right?" He heard Ma say the words, looking up at him in concern.

However, he couldn't put together the words to answer her. His mind was one hundred percent occupied by the woman staring at him from across the room with wide eyes as dark as the night sky.

For a moment, he thought that he would turn around and run right then and there, but then she was moving toward him. Before he could get his mind in order, she was repeating his name again.

Goodness, the way she said it was either a sin or a prayer, he couldn't tell which. Her voice almost plunged him into memories he had long since buried, and he had to breathe in deeply through his nose to stay in the moment.

She was even more beautiful than his memory told him. Her body had filled out with her womanhood, her hourglass figure no doubt tempting many a man to think things they wouldn't want their mother to overhear. Her hair was long and a glossy obsidian, done up in a braided crown about her head, as if she needed further proof of her naturally royal elegance. Her features were aquiline, blending into each other like they were carefully painted by a master artist. Those ruby red, full lips were parted slightly in her query, and her rounded cheeks were flushed the faintest pink.

What was that expression on her face? Hopeful? Happy? Upset? He couldn't tell, his mind was so occupied in observing every minute detail about her that he could.

What is she doing here? He couldn't help but wonder. She's supposed to be almost a continent away.

She said his name one more time, and his mother gently elbowed him, stirring him back to reality and the woman who was standing before him.

"Actually, it's Ben now."

There. That was neutral. Neutral was good. He wasn't

screaming at her and asking how dare she come back after breaking his heart, and he wasn't mocking her for being back. He wasn't falling to his knees and begging her to come back to him.

"Oh. Right, of course. I suppose it would be weird for a grown man to go by the name Benny."

"It would."

Thankfully, Ben's mother stepped forward and offered her hand. "Hello dear, how are you?"

"Not the best," she answered with a wan smile. It was hard to stay mad or aggressive with her, considering the situation. They were at her father's funeral, and although Ben didn't know if they'd had a chance to reconcile since she left them, he figured it was a difficult situation nonetheless. "But I'm glad to be here so Mom's not alone."

"Oh, you don't have to worry about Ruby, dear. She's got all of us to care for her."

"I know." Although she was talking with Ben's mother, her eyes kept flicking to Ben.

So dark and focused that they were almost pitch black, he had no idea how she was able to convey so much emotion with only a glance. He remembered how those same eyes looked as they gazed up at him with affection, the stars in the sky above reflecting in the pools of onyx.

"But I want to be here for her. It's been a long time since I've visited, and I figured... well... I've already put it off long enough."

"Well, it's lovely to see you back in town again. If you need anything, you just let us know. I'd love to hear all about New York!"

"Hah, that's definitely a story."

"I'm sure. Oh, and I brought some food for you," Ma said

before quickly continuing on. "You don't have to worry about telling me where to put it. Unfortunately, I've had enough of these events lately that I know to put it in the other room."

"Ah, I see. Thank you. And, um... I'm sorry?"

"Dear no, you don't have to apologize to me. That's the consolation prize for getting to my age. But today is about your father."

It was all too much. Standing there, looking at the woman who snapped his heart into so many pieces was impossibly painful. It made him want to curl into a ball, or punch a wall, or go for a horse ride until the sun set and all of his frantic thoughts went away.

"Excuse me," he heard himself say. "I think I left the windows open in the truck."

With that, he turned on his heel and quickly walked out. But as fast as he strode, he couldn't outwalk the memories that were flooding his mind.

"So what college are you going to? Have you filled out any applications?"

There she was, laying on a blanket beside him, the sun shining down while the tall grass waved all around them. He could still smell the lavender shampoo in her hair and the vanilla hand lotion she always used. It was burned into his mind for all eternity.

"Actually, I don't think I'm gonna. There are a few tradesmen in town who are willing to teach me what I need to know to keep the ranch running smoothly, so I figure I might as well save the money."

She sat up suddenly, giving him a curious look. "You're not going to college?"

He knew her well enough to recognize that was not a good

tone. "Yeah. Just seems like it would be a waste of money since I'm going to be taking over the ranch."

"Oh... I thought..."

"You thought what?"

"That we would be going together. You know, get out of this place and actually experience something other than Blackfish County."

Oh.

Oh no.

Sure, they had daydreamed about running away from the small town and all the small minds that surrounded them, but to him those had always been starry-eyed stories that they used to vent and cope with the drama of being teenagers.

"You've always known that I was going to take over the ranch. I'm the eldest."

"Who cares if you're the eldest. You're my boyfriend! No one's saying you can't come back here, just that you could at least experience some of the world before deciding that this is your destiny for the rest of your life."

"I want to help run the ranch. I know you hate this town, but I don't. I like seeing the animals every day. I like growing things and building with my own two hands. I don't want to spend thousands of dollars on college when I can learn what I need to know from experienced workers here in town."

"What do we do then?" The way she looked at him, so heart-broken and betrayed, it made him feel like he was in the wrong. But what was so bad about loving his family and the life they provided?

"I... I don't know."

"Dang it, Chastity," Ben hissed to himself, slapping the roof of his truck. Normally, he wasn't one to hit anything—not a lot made him angry enough to physically react. But there were so many emotions running through him that he needed some way to get them out, and his trusty gelding Manchester wasn't around for a good run.

He heard light footsteps behind him and whipped around, almost expecting to see her appear out of thin air. But thankfully it wasn't the specter of his past, but instead his mother, looking quite concerned.

"Did you know that she would be here?" he asked, gathering his thoughts enough to form a coherent sentence.

"No, darling," she answered, laying her wizened hand on his arm. "I sincerely thought she was still busy galivanting around in the city. Ruby never told me that she was expecting her back."

Ben relaxed, heaving a large sigh and leaning against his truck. Despite the uncanny coincidence, he did believe his mother. She was never one to lie, and he knew she would have asked his younger brother Benji instead if she thought there was any chance of Chastity being around.

"You know, it has been a long time..."

Ben looked over to his mother, who was gazing up at him with a soft expression. It seemed that no matter how old he was, she'd always have an eye out for him.

"It's been years, but I still feel it like it was yesterday."

"Aye, first loves are often that way. They can completely change how you look at the world."

"I guess that's what happened to me. Are you ready to go?"

She hesitated as if she wanted to say something more, so Ben waited patiently for her to get the words out. "Is it really so bad that she's back in town?"

He thought about it, trying to rifle through all of the frantic and disjointed ideas going through his head. But in the end, he was caught somewhere between happy and horrified at her sudden appearance.

"I guess I don't know, Ma."

"That's fair."

She reached up to pat his cheek, and he opened the truck door for her. Once she was in, he shut the door then headed to his own side. Without a single look behind him, he turned on the vehicle and sped out of there—perhaps a little faster than he should have. But as he drove, he couldn't help but look in his rearview mirror. Whether he wanted to see Chastity's reflection appear there or not was a mystery even to his own self.

6

Chastity

*C*hastity stood there, staring at the air where Ben had just been standing. Had she really just seen her high school sweetheart? The first and only man to hold her heart for any length of time.

Even after all these years, she knew it was him. It was like her body had sensed him and whipped her head in his direction, drinking him in like a tall glass of water that she was so incredibly thirsty for.

No!

Stop that!

She couldn't afford to think about him that way. Now was a time to be hard—to be strong. She had trusted him with everything once, and then he had gone back on his word, blaming it all on her.

She wouldn't be the villain in this story. She had way too many important things to do.

...even if he was still as drop-dead gorgeous as ever.

She couldn't say what she liked the most about him. Whether it was his strong jaw, or the serious way in which he gazed at people. Or maybe it was his rumbling bass of a laugh. Who knew? Was it possible to be even more attracted to him— even after a decade apart?

...It seemed so.

How uncanny.

Shaking her head, Chastity forced her mind back on track. With everything that had been going on, she hadn't even thought about him coming to the wake. But of course, he would. Events like this were often town-wide events. She should have known better.

Maybe her subconscious had figured that he would hate her forever and never want to have anything to do with her family again.

"But I don't understand why you have to go."

He was staring at her with those intoxicating green eyes again, his strong, thick brows knit together with concern. She stood on her porch, an acceptance letter in each hand, feeling shocked by his displeased reaction.

"But I've told you about my dream for years. We even talked about a way to make it work with you staying here and me getting my degree."

"I thought you would change your mind since you've been doing so poorly this semester."

"I had meningitis! But I'd already sent my transcripts and everything else to colleges. They don't know about this semester's grades because we haven't gotten them yet."

He stared at her, and she could tell his heart was breaking, but she didn't want any part of it. "Why won't you stay with me?"

"I can't," Chastity answered, her voice cracking. "Please don't make me choose between you and what I've always dreamed of."

"Are you all right, sweetie?"

Chastity pulled herself from her unpleasant memory, wiping at her eyes. How selfish. Her father was dead, and they were literally at his wake, yet she was making this all about some silly romance from when she was sixteen. It seemed that skipping two years of school through advanced placement hadn't prepared her for such emotional troubles.

"I'm fine," she answered, calming down and forcing herself to put on the correct face. "It was just Benny. Ben, I mean. Ben Miller."

"Oh, is that one of your friends from the city? Did you not come alone?"

Chastity gave her a curious look, raising one of her eyebrows. "What do you mean, Mom? You know who Ben is."

"Do I? The name doesn't ring a bell."

"How can it not? He was my boyfriend for three years. We met in sophomore year when I didn't have any friends because everyone thought I was weird for liking to read for fun and watching old movies. He took me under his wing in our advanced math class and things kinda went from there? We were in Mathletics together."

It was true. Chastity could vividly remember eating lunch by herself for all of freshmen year and then part of sophomore year until Ben had just so happened to accidentally knock over her milk. He apologized and ran to get paper towels, one thing led to another and, somehow, they ended up talking about the slew of comic book movie adaptions from the sixties.

Eventually the bell had rung, and they had gone their separate ways, but the next day she couldn't help but wonder if he would be there again. Against all hope, she had slid into her usual seat in the library with a book in front of her, only to have him slide into the seat across from her.

From there they had basically been inseparable in their free periods. After a month or so of that, they ended up in Mathletics together. At first most of the team had been surprised by Ben's appearance. He was a popular kid and had a lot going for him, and most people assumed he was taking over the lucrative Miller Ranch, so he certainly didn't need the college credits. Strangely, he had insisted on only being partnered with Chastity for their pre-competition practices, because, apparently, she was "the only person that he really knew"—or that was what he'd said.

At first, she had wondered if it was some sort of elaborate scheme, especially when he wasn't really that great at math, but after long enough it became clear that he had joined just to spend time with her. So she let herself relax and then their after-school hours were filled with each other too. Then they started hanging out even after that, taking turns going to each other's houses for dinner.

But it wasn't until she was fifteen, a year after they had met, when her parents finally gave her permission to date him.

That was a whole lot of history. Countless nights holding hands and staring up at the sky, dreaming together, confiding in each other. Chastity's father had always joked about how he was the best son-in-law he could have asked for.

So how could Mom not remember?

But then another person was stepping forward and pulling her into a hug. Chastity barely paid attention, going through the motions as she watched her mother react.

Her mom was still teary, and Chastity didn't think that would stop for a while, but she responded to almost everyone by name and seemed to know who they were. Perhaps she too only thought of Ben as Benny, and since she was so stressed, her mind wasn't making the connection.

Yeah, that was plausible.

...right?

Chastity found herself wishing she had been around her more, because then she would know if this was normal or not. Three years was far too long to have left her parents alone, and she wondered for how long that guilt would plague her by manifesting as other things. Such as the paranoia that she was feeling right now.

But try as she might to dismiss it, a shiver went down her spine. Something in her gut was telling her that something wasn't right. There was no way her mother could forget about Ben, the man who had held Chastity's heart during her most formative years. The man who was her first kiss. And her first heartbreak. The man she had built so many dreams with, only to have all of them amount to nothing.

Goodness knew Chastity couldn't forget.

7

Chastity

"*M*om! Are you ready?"

Chastity looked up the stairs as she called out, glancing at her watch for the tenth time that morning.

Three days since the wake, and it seemed like life hadn't stopped spinning yet. From the moment the wake had ended, she and her mom had to deal with getting all the food home, picking up her father's ashes, and handling tons of well-meaning phone calls.

Chastity worried that perhaps she was being cold. She hadn't cried since the wake, and she'd spent most of her time attending to everything that needed to be done. But how could she give herself time to mourn when there was so much to do? She tried to remember if she had ever had to deal with a death in the family before, wondering if this was maybe just how her mind mourned things, but the only person who she remembered passing was a grandmother who lived on the reservation. It had been a sad affair, but Chastity had only met her once. Apparently, the older woman didn't like that her daughter had married someone not from the tribe and had never really gotten over that.

Huh. It seemed strained familial issues ran in the bloodline. But Chastity tucked those negative thoughts away and tried to focus on the good things while she cleaned the house. It really was amazing how much food the town had poured out for them. Even after three days, the fridge was stuffed to bursting with all sorts of perishables, ranging from pies to casseroles, to fresh roasts. Chastity was sure she had even seen a couple of different types of pulled pork in there.

It didn't stop there. On the shelves was all the stuff that didn't need to keep cool, like dozens of cans of vegetables, bags of potatoes, applesauce, chips and other guilty snacks, cans of soup, and all sorts of dried fruits. It seemed the town really wanted to make sure that Ruby didn't go hungry or cook for herself until she was ready.

But while all of that was good, wonderful even, there was something else that wasn't so great.

Mom never ended up remembering Ben, and several strange things she did the day after the wake had bothered Chastity. She couldn't really say why, she knew that there was something... *off.*

Thankfully, on Monday, she was able to call right at nine in the morning and get a doctor's appointment for the next day. Sometimes there really were perks to living in a small town.

But now that it was finally time for her appointment, her mom was being a bit stubborn.

"I'm telling you, this really isn't necessary."

"I know, Mom," Chastity said gently, going to the top of the stairs and offering her arm to her mother. Her seemingly fragile mother took it, and they slowly went down the steps. "But I haven't seen you in three years, so please humor me. Consider this just making sure we start my visit on the right foot."

"Yes, because the death of your father is the right foot."

Chastity blushed a bit at that. Her mother certainly had a point. But even though it was a gentle chide, it was good to hear her mother's quick—yet subtle sense of humor return. "You know what I mean."

"Yes, I do." She reached up to pat Chastity's head, and they headed out the door. Just like everything else in town, it was only about a ten-minute walk to wherever they needed to go.

"I'm going to miss him so much, Maryanne."

Chastity almost stopped dead in her tracks but managed to keep putting one foot in front of the other.

"Pardon me?"

"Charlie. He's gone now, and I'm just... not sure what to do. We've been together for so long, I can't imagine a life without him, Maryanne."

There it was again. Part of her mind was torn in the direction of her poor mother missing Father so terribly, but the other was wrapped up in why the heck her mom was calling her by her *grandmother's* name?

"Do you think I'm Maryanne right now?" Chastity asked cautiously, trying to sound casual, which was difficult considering that the sliver of uncertainty that had been niggling around her mind was now a full-blown cold feeling in the pit of her stomach.

"Of course. Who else would you be?"

"That's right," she licked her lips, trying to pick her words carefully. "I'm Maryanne." Another pause before she took a deep breath. "Where's Chastity, by the way?"

Now it was her mother's turn to sigh. "In the city. I don't think she's ever coming back. Sometimes I don't know if we're even from the same world. I want to understand her, but... but sometimes it seems like I can't. I just want her to be happy. And to be safe. The city is so dangerous!"

Ow.

Chastity's heart throbbed, and it took everything in her to keep her breath from catching. There was something utterly disarming about hearing her mother confess to how tenuous their relationship was. It seemed that they both wanted to love each other but had no idea how.

"Oh look, we're already here."

Chastity looked up to see the familiar front of the doctor's office. Somehow it looked completely untouched by time, as if a single day hadn't passed since she'd gotten her checkup before she rushed off to college. The handymen who kept up the place must have been exceptionally on-task over the years for it to still look so good.

They strolled inside, and from there, they waited in the reception area. Chastity's mind went to all the memories that were woven into the walls around her. She had been treated for strep here, and the flu, and then that incredibly unpleasant bout of meningitis. So many coughs, gags, and weary wheezes.

Eventually, the nurse called her mother's name, and Chastity rose automatically to go with her. However, Ruby seemed to have some other ideas, because she turned and sharply regarded her daughter. "What are you doing?"

"Going with you."

"I'm a grown woman. I can handle myself."

And with that she was off behind the doors with the nurse.

Chastity's teeth worried at her lip as she watched the door like a hawk. How was she going to explain what was going on with her mother if she wasn't in the room with the doctor? She was sure that this was some sort of HIPAA violation.

Chastity's phone buzzed. She looked at the screen to see a text from her agent. *When are you coming back to NY?*

She fired off a quick response. Not sure. There are complications. Why?

The response made her heart sink. Open auditions for a new show next week.

Chastity frowned as she responded. Shoot. Won't be able to make it. Taking care of my mother.

The sound of a door opening caused Chastity to look up, and she was surprised to see that same nurse there. "Miss Parker?"

Chastity found herself on her feet instantly, trying to keep her expression neutral. She was afraid that if she emoted, all of the worry within her would burst out at once.

"Yes?" she managed to squeak out without sounding like a terrified mouse.

"Mrs. Parker has you added as her power of attorney, correct?"

"Yes," Chastity answered, swallowing hard.

Those were words she hadn't heard in a long time. Her mom had designated Chastity to make medical decisions on her behalf if she were ever to become too sick or mentally unfit to declare her own desires. Why on earth would that be relevant now?

"We'd like to talk to you, if you don't mind."

Chastity nodded and followed after her, being led into the back. The nurse took her to a patient room, leaving her there with a comment that the doctor would be in soon.

Why did they have her in here? Why was she separate from her mother? Why did they ask about the power of attorney?

Finally, the doctor stepped in, calmly shutting the door behind him. He was just as she remembered him, but with white touching his temples. Perhaps he had crow's-feet, whereas he had none before, but other than that it was like stepping into a time machine.

"Ms. Parker?" he asked, even though he had to know who she was.

"Yes," Chastity answered automatically, still struggling to keep her voice steady. "Did you need something? I have my mom's insurance card."

"No, no, Ms. Parker, it's not that." He paused, as if considering exactly how to phrase the next sentence out of his mouth. "Your mother is sick, Ms. Parker. I can't exactly be sure with what, as we don't have the right things here to test her. I'm recommending that you take her to a doctor in the city who has the appropriate equipment to diagnose and treat her."

"Sick?" Chastity repeated, her eyes going wide. "With what? Do you mean cancer?"

"No, no nothing like that." The doctor took off his glasses a moment and rubbed at his nose before placing them back on. "But still serious. I don't like throwing these words around lightly, but I believe she is exhibiting signs of dementia, or Alzheimer's. I'm recommending you to this doctor, so they can distinguish which, but also because they specialize in treatment regarding elderly mental care."

"Dementia."

It seemed like the world had curled itself into a spiral, shrinking down to a spinning web of awful. Chastity could hear her heart in her ears, thundering through her veins, and suddenly she felt so very alone.

"There is a chance that it could be something else. I'm by no means an expert in this area, but the symptoms point me in this direction. I really, really urge you to make an appointment." He handed her a card, and Chastity took it in her shaking hands. "She may resist. She thinks she's fine, but it's important that you don't listen to her. I'm sure you've already noticed the signs, and her probable denial of them."

Chastity nodded, and he stepped aside to open the door. "She's in the room across the way if you want to collect her and head out. Of course, take as much time as you need."

Chastity couldn't speak, so she only nodded dully as she stepped out into the hall. The doctor made a polite gesture to the opposite door then walked to the front, giving her a bit of privacy.

Which she sorely needed.

Chastity slumped against the wall, her world still spinning. Her mother was sick? She had hoped that the suspicious feeling in her gut had only been paranoia, but now that those fears had been proven true, she didn't feel any better.

She had just lost her father and was still struggling with how she felt about that. She couldn't lose her mother too. Nor could she watch her mom slowly waste away as whatever illness she had ate away at what made her...well, *her*.

While Chastity hadn't had any direct experience with dementia or Alzheimer's, she knew people who had. They were cruel, debilitating diseases that stole away memories, personalities, and happiness until there was little left.

She didn't want that for her mother, so she prayed that whatever was going on with her was something else entirely.

Steadying herself, she took a deep breath then headed for the door, knocking slightly.

"Hey there, you ready to head home?" she asked, looking over to her mother.

The woman brightened, smiling at her daughter, and

Chastity couldn't help but return the smile. She had been looking forward to trying to repair her strained relationship with her remaining parent, but what if that chance was stolen away before she even had the opportunity to make amends?

Was this her punishment? Had she done something wrong? Because she had taken her parents and her hometown for granted, were they going to be ripped from her forever?

"Something wrong, Maryanne?"

"Not really. I'm just—" Chastity stopped, catching the comment. "Am I still Maryanne?"

"You ask the silliest questions," Chasity's mom stated before she stood and offered her an arm. "Let's go home, shall we?"

"Yeah, that sounds like a good idea."

Chastity offered her arm, stomach through the floor, as they headed out again. Her mother kept up a good conversation the entire short walk to their house, but not once did she ever use Chastity's name.

It was upsetting, and Chastity did her hardest not to show it, but her mother seemed to sense something was amiss. Once she was in the door, her mother spoke of needing a nap and then headed up the stairs.

Chastity was pleased to see that she could still get up there on her own, but it was a very small victory. Once her mother was out of sight, she went back outside onto the porch to call the city doctor.

Of course, she was on hold forever, and when she finally did get to speak with a secretary, the woman told her that the doctor wasn't accepting any new patients for a year. That had nearly cut Chastity through, and she had to hold all of her emotions inside of herself not to blow up on the phone.

She dropped the referring doctor's name and mentioned that her mother needed testing for diagnosis and treatment as soon as possible. That seemed to do something, and the woman stated they would call her back after speaking to the referring doctor. It didn't take long, and the doctor must have sounded convincing of her need for treatment, because the lady offered a round of appointments the next day for all the tests she needed. She also told Chastity that her mother needed to fast overnight for a blood test.

Chastity told her thank you and wrote down the appointment times, but when she hung up a whole new set of problems alighted on her.

She didn't have a car, and neither did her mother. She had to get her mom a ride into the city, but it was thirty miles away. There wasn't even a bus that ran that way and taking a train there would certainly be expensive. Too expensive for her budget, and she wasn't sure of her mother's yet.

Perhaps her mother had a friend that could take them?

Going back into the house, Chastity went over to her mother's desk, rooting around for something that might help. She wasn't sure how much time she wasted going through drawers when she finally spotted an old address book on one of the higher parts of the desk.

Oh.

She grabbed that and went through it page by page. She recognized several of her mother's old friends but knew that a few of them had already passed away, just like her father.

Finally, she came upon a name she recognized. *Annie.* It had a pleasant sort of ring to it, so Chastity guessed that she probably knew who this person was, from when she was younger maybe.

Picking up the phone, she dialed the number. It rang twice, then a gentle voice came over the phone.

"Hello?"

"Oh, hi. Annie?"

"This is she, who do I have the pleasure of speaking with?"

"This is Chastity, Mrs. Parker's daughter."

"Oh, Chastity! Hello! I remember you."

Oh. How awkward. Chastity could only vaguely remember that she might have known a Mrs. Annie at one point. "Really? Well, that makes this easier. I was calling to ask a favor of you."

"Of course, dear. I'm so sorry about your father's passing. I know how much he and your mother were in love."

"...yeah. They were." Chastity took a deep breath, wondering if she was violating her mother's privacy. But she didn't see much of an option. "Well, the reason I'm calling is because my mother needs to go to a doctor in the city for some specialized tests and neither of us have a car."

"Oh goodness, tests? Is she all right?"

Chastity's stomach did that drop again. She hated it. "I don't know."

Somehow the woman seemed to sense her tone and feeling over the phone. "I'll have one of my sons take the two of you, don't worry about a thing. What time do you need him there tomorrow?"

"Thank you. I think nine a.m. should do. Do you need the address?"

She laughed lightly, and it was a warm, comforting sound. "Oh darling, I helped your mother move into that house back when we were both young women. I know exactly where it is.

"Please, rest up and get some sleep. You're not alone in this, Chastity. You have the whole town behind you."

"...thanks." Chastity didn't know what to say to that. There was an inherent sort of niceness to her tone, and it made the situation feel less hopeless. "I appreciate that."

"Of course, dear. If you need anything else, just let me know."

"I will."

She hung up, leaving Chastity staring at the wall. Sure, the situation was awful, but at least the people here were so much closer than people back in the city. If this had happened back in the Big Apple, she was sure that she would be more overwhelmed.

Hopefully, that closeness didn't backfire on her somehow.

8

Ben

*B*en gently pressed his heels into his horse's side, deciding another fifteen minutes of riding wasn't going to hurt anyone. The workers were finishing tending to the animals, and his brother had asked for a break from renovating the barn they were working on, so the ranch wouldn't suffer if he took a little time to clear his head.

He rode past the dozens of hay bales they had, taking a deep breath of the twilight air as the sun sank behind the horizon. He loved this time of day. There weren't the dangers that came with darkness, but there was the quiet of the world starting to tuck itself in for slumber. It made it easier to think, the pressing list of responsibilities in his head fading for a few hours.

Not that he hadn't been thinking all day, just not about anything he was supposed to be concerned with. Ever since he had seen Chastity, his mind had lingered on her, replaying every second of their interaction on a loop.

The way she looked. The way she smelled. The curl of her full lips; the uncertain look in her eyes. Did she fear him? Was she ashamed? He couldn't tell. It had been so long since he had seen her that he had lost the ability to read her emotions. Once he had prided himself on knowing her like the back of his hand. Now she was practically a stranger.

Albeit a stranger who he felt inexplicably tied to in a way he couldn't explain.

Ben tried to harden his mind, trying to suppress the rising emotions. Chastity had made it clear her life belonged far away from here, and he was rooted right where he was.

...but was he okay with that?

He didn't know.

Taking over the ranch as the eldest had always been a matter of course, but she'd made him question it before—and now he was again. Perhaps there was more for him beyond tending to the animals, barns, and dozens of other responsibilities that came with farm life.

His horse, Gertie, let out a whinny, drawing him back to reality.

"Come on, Ben," he said to himself. "Snap out of it."

He loved the ranch. He loved working with his hands and carrying on the legacy that had been so lovingly built for him. He loved that they specialized in happy animals, and though they didn't replicate on a massive scale, it felt more like how God wanted humans to respect beasts of burden and livestock.

Why would he ever give that up to go to some stone-cold city where he had to work to make some other man rich? It seemed more like torture than a dream, and he didn't think he would ever understand Chastity's need to get away.

But he didn't need to understand her, he told himself. Chastity was practically like a stranger now, and what she did was none of his business. It didn't matter if she was back in town for her father's funeral, she would be gone soon, leaving only a shadow and a memory.

Oh, and that empty feeling that was growing again in his chest.

Ben *tsked* to himself and pointed Gertie back to the riding barn. It was becoming clear that no matter how far or fast he rode, he wasn't going to get his peace tonight.

How was she still affecting him this way? It'd been years of no contact, and she'd barely said ten words to him, yet he felt like she had left all over again. How stupid. He had too much to do to be worried about some high school love that hadn't panned out.

Once Gertie was all taken care of, brushed, watered, and fed, he headed toward the main house. Normally, he could just go in his own door, but he was hoping maybe his ma was inside or even one of his brothers. For some reason, he didn't really want to be alone.

It wasn't because he didn't want to think about Chastity. Or at least that was what he repeated to himself several times. It wasn't because of the electricity that had crackled between them when their eyes met. And it wasn't because he felt like he was obsessing over her now.

Ma was sitting in the living room, this time doing a cross-stitch as she rocked in her chair. She looked like the quintessential Western mother, humming to herself as she rocked.

"Hey there," Ben said, crossing over to her and flopping onto their sofa. She gave him a look, never having succeeded in thirty years in getting him to stop throwing himself onto their furniture. Hey, he was a hard worker and the eldest, but he never said that he was perfect. "What are you up to tonight?"

"Oh, nothing," she said, but Ben caught there was something odd in her tone. "I'm thinking about a friend who needs some help in town."

"Really?" Ben asked curiously. He wasn't sure what about it was piquing his interest, but he knew that something was up. "What do they need?"

"Ah, well she is having some medical issues and needs to go into the city for some special tests. They asked if we would be able to give them a ride, and I told them I would be more than happy to send them one of my brood. It's the Christian thing to do, you know?"

Ben chuckled. "Of course, it is. You always love to help people, even at your own detriment."

"What are you talking about? I think that helping people only ever helps myself."

"Uh-huh. Remember when you broke your wrist helping someone with a busted tire on the side of the road when I was five?"

"Well yes, but they got home in time to see their daughter at her recital, didn't they?"

Ben sighed, shaking his head. Maybe one day he would be as kind and giving as his ma.

"Fair enough. Who is it? I'm probably free."

"Uh, I don't know if that's the best idea."

That made Ben's head snap up, and he studied his mother's face. Something was definitely going on. Why did she look so guilty? The tiny, cold, tail end of an idea tickled at the back of his head, and he regarded her suspiciously.

"Who is this *friend*, Ma?"

"Mrs. Parker. Chastity's mother."

Several emotions raced through Ben's mind all at once, and he wondered which ones flashed across his face. Most likely the angry one considering his mother's expression.

Chastity's mother was sick? Was it bad? It had to be if she was going all the way into the city. How horrible, to come home to the loss of her father and then have something happen with her mother. Maybe—

He cut off that thought. No. He wasn't worried about her. It was sad, but none of his business. Chastity had made sure of that.

"I would never ask you to do it. I was planning on calling up Benji, but his phone's been off all day."

"Yeah, he messed it up last night when he dropped it in the toilet," Ben answered, rubbing his temples. "He has one coming in the mail, but it probably won't be here until tomorrow."

"Oh, well if you would be so kind, you could ride over to his place and ask him—"

"No, it's fine." Despite the clamor in his head that said he shouldn't get involved, Ben decided to be the bigger person. Maybe he was a bit more like his mother than he thought. If Mrs. Parker needed help and he could provide it, it wouldn't be very Christian to duck out of it.

"What time do they need me there tomorrow?"

"She said about nine a.m. It is a bit of a drive, and it sounds like there are quite a few tests to do. Thank you, Ben. I really didn't expect you to do this. I didn't even plan on telling you."

"I know," he answered with a sigh. "You always try to look out for all of us, even though we're grown men."

"You may be grown, but you're still all my baby boys."

"Your baby boys have all been taller than you since we were twelve."

"The day that height becomes the cut off for maternal affection is the day I throw myself from a cliff." She yawned and set her things to the side. "Well, now that I'm not worried about how to contact Benji, I think I'll go have a lie down. Your father is already sleeping. He chopped some wood earlier and it wiped him right out."

"The man has five sons and twelve workers. He really doesn't need to be out cutting firewood for himself."

"A man is a man is a man. Even at his age, he likes to do things for himself. I figured you would understand that more than anyone."

"Yeah, I guess I do. Goodnight, Ma." Ben stood to kiss her forehead, and she patted his broad shoulder lovingly. With that, she tottered off, leaving him alone with his thoughts once again.

Tomorrow was going to be awkward, stilted, and unpleasant, but at least he was doing the right thing and helping out a couple of people in need. Now that they were grown adults and had moved on, there was no reason why they couldn't be friends.

Even if Ben was beginning to suspect that he hadn't moved on at all.

9

Ben

Ben's leg bounced as he drove his truck into town. It wasn't that far of a drive, but it was far enough to give his mind the time to think way too much. He wasn't sure how he was supposed to act around Chastity. Would he be cold and detached? Maybe the silent treatment? Would he be friendly and act as if nothing was wrong?

Well, probably not that last one. While no one really called him *mean* as far as he knew, he wasn't exactly the life of the party. A lot of different words had been used to describe him. Taciturn. Stoic. Reserved. Responsible. None of those really meant *great at conversation,* or *comfortable around forced interaction with his ex.*

He pulled up to their house, just off the main drag, and he realized that he was going to have to decide fast. He knew he didn't want to be openly hostile, but he didn't want Chastity to think that this was some pathetic way to get back with her.

No, he just wanted to help. He wasn't sure if it was some left-over feeling of protection he had for Chastity, or his natural inclination to be responsible, or even an attempt to follow his mother's selfless examples, but he supposed the reason *why* didn't really matter now that he was at his destination.

The front door opened and Ben stepped out of the truck to help. It was an extended cab, so there was more than enough room for the three of them, but since it was so large, by the time he did get around, Chastity had already led her mother right up to the passenger's side.

She stopped dead in her tracks when she saw him, as if she was staring at a ghost. Ben was a bit confused by her surprise. But then it started to dawn on him that maybe she didn't realize it was *his* mother that she was calling for help. That certainly made things a little awkward.

"What are you doing here?" she sputtered.

Ben couldn't help but feel insulted. They hadn't ended on the best of terms, but even standing ten feet away from her he could feel that strange force pulling them together, but that didn't mean she needed to stare at him like he was some sort of specter.

"You asked my mother for a ride. She doesn't drive much anymore, so here I am."

"Oh... Annie is *your* mother?"

"Yes. Did you forget?"

She shrugged, still staring at him as he carefully approached to open the passenger door and help her mother in. "I guess I did. I don't think I ever called her anything other than 'Mrs. Miller.' Doesn't your dad call her 'pumpkin' all the time, or something?"

Ben couldn't help but grin at that. Pumpkin was a long running joke from his parents first date where his mom had unfortunately found out that she had a severe allergy to pumpkins. Instead of enjoying pumpkin cider at a high school Halloween dance, they'd spent their night in the ER. It wasn't a typical romance story, but they were still together and clearly in love, so something must have turned out right.

"Yeah. He does call her that. If I make you uncomfortable, I can get one of my brothers, but then you might be late."

"No!" she objected a little forcefully and seemed to even surprise herself. "I mean, no, it's fine. I'm sorry if I reacted poorly. You're just possibly the last person I expected to see. Thank you. I really do appreciate this."

She gave Ben a sheepish sort of look and it was hard for him to keep his heart from melting at the sight. How her dark eyes could always convey so much emotion still amazed him. They were far too easy to drown in, so he just tipped his head down, so he didn't have to look at them.

"Apology accepted."

Mrs. Parker leaned out of her seat between Ben and Chastity, looking amused. "Are we going to get on the road for these silly tests that I don't really need, or just lollygag in the street all day?"

"Sorry, Mom. Just having a chat. We'll be leaving shortly."

"I don't think we need to go at all. I'm just humoring you because I haven't seen you in forever."

"Thanks, Mom."

Chastity's gaze flicked to Ben in embarrassment, and he asked in a whisper if her mom really was sick. She nodded, giving him his answer. Well, that was that. He went to go to the driver's seat, but paused for a moment, wondering if he should help Chastity into the back seat like he had aided her mother into the front, but Chastity was in the car before he could come to a conclusion.

At least that much hadn't changed. Even from a young age, Chastity had always been independent.

Ben supposed that was why they ultimately went their separate ways.

Shaking that thought from his head, he went back around the truck and got in. As the engine came to life, it made him feel better. If anyone tried to draw him into a conversation, he could just comment that he needed to concentrate on driving.

He headed toward the main road and out of town when he heard Mrs. Parker begin to address him.

"You look familiar, young man. Do I know you? And more importantly, do you know my daughter, Chastity? She's single, you know."

"Mother!"

Ben couldn't help when the corner of his mouth curled into a smirk at first. It seemed that it was a mother's job everywhere to humiliate their children. But then another part of her statement sunk in. Did she not recognize him? He was aware that he had grown taller since his high school days where he would spend hours studying on their couch, but he was sure that he was distinguishable as Benedict Miller.

"Don't you remember me, Mrs. Parker?"

She blinked at him, clearly confused. "Why would I recognize a cab driver?"

"A cab dri—" Ben cut himself off, his eyes flicking to the rearview mirror to glance at Chastity. Her face had gone pale, and her eyes were firmly set upon her mother.

Oh.

It seemed she really was sick.

A sinking feeling filled Ben's stomach as he realized what

the situation might be. He fervently hoped and prayed it wasn't the case, but he remembered when Auntie McKenzie's mind started to go. It had been a terrible process, and in the end, she only recognized one of her daughters. He hated to think of Chastity having to go through that.

Lord, please let it be something curable by these doctors, he prayed to himself.

"This is Ben Miller," Chastity said slowly, as if she wasn't sure that she should be correcting her mother at all or letting her stay in whatever reality she had at the moment. "You remember him from my high school days, right?"

"Ben? Ben Miller... I..." Mrs. Parker seemed to think about it, and then her eyes lit up. "Ah yes! He was the boy that you used to be head over heels in love with and the two of you were planning on running away together, right?"

Because of course she would say that.

The truck was silent for a moment with Mrs. Parker just blinking expectantly, like she didn't understand what she had done. Ben wasn't about to touch that with a ten-foot pole, so after what felt like a full minute, Chastity cleared her throat.

"Yeah. Used to."

For some reason, those three words stung much more than they should have.

10

Chastity

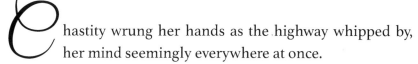Chastity wrung her hands as the highway whipped by, her mind seemingly everywhere at once.

Of course, it was Ben who would come and get her. Because that's what life liked to do to her. And of course, her mother would have a moment of lucidity concerning the man where she would remember that they had once been an item.

It made far too many memories and feelings pop up. Ones that she had long stuffed deep down in her heart or shoved to the back of her head in her desperate march to pay the bills while constantly being broke.

When she was younger, she had been such a hopeless romantic. It had taken a decade in the city to hammer those tendencies out, but now she found them rising to the surface again. How ridiculous! She was a grown woman, but she was letting herself get butterflies over a man who—until very, very recently—she had assumed she would never see again.

Thankfully the conversation lulled for the rest of the ride, her mother instead humming ditties along with the radio. While the quiet gave Chastity too much time to think, at least it didn't force her into conversation with the man who had almost managed to keep her from following her dreams—the dreams that weren't *exactly* panning out like she had hoped.

Ben parked and went around the car like a gentleman, opening Chastity's car door first but thankfully not physically helping her out. That he saved for her mother, whom he gently assisted out of his tall truck and onto the ground.

It seemed that much hadn't changed. She remembered watching him with newborn lambs or little chicks. He always had such a gentle spirit to him despite his rugged cowboy ways.

Her gaze flicked to his hands as he guided his mother gently inside of the doctor's office. She remembered those hands on her back when they were younger. They had always tried to play things carefully and honor God by not passing over a certain line, but they had certainly made out like there was no tomorrow. What an awkward thing to think while her mother was tottering into a strange doctor's office.

Thankfully, those thoughts fell off as they headed inside, and she helped her mom check in. She wanted once again to accompany her mother to the room, but once more was told by her mother that she didn't need Chasity to go in with her. Since she wasn't documented as being unable to take care of herself and was lucid at the moment, Chastity found herself relegated to the waiting room.

She sat down in a chair, her leg bouncing, and Ben sat several seats away from her. It wasn't as harsh as plopping himself down on the opposite side of the room, but it spoke to just how far apart they were now.

She shouldn't have to feel guilty for following her dreams. Her parents had never really believed in her, with old fashioned ideas about how she should be married and have kids because that was the best destiny a woman could hope for. The ultimate fulfillment of her design as a female.

It wasn't that Chastity hated the thought of marriage or kids or any of that stuff, but she resented the fact that her parents thought that was the pinnacle of her potential. She could touch the moon, discover new planets, cure cancer, anything really, but they didn't seem to believe or care about that. Her father had even gone so far as to tell her that taking all of those advanced classes was a waste of time and the only need to go to college was for her "Mrs." degree.

So, of course, she had to get away. She had thought that Ben understood that and would come with her. Sure, maybe they would return to his ranch later and help run things, but they would experience all of the things that weren't in their small town. They would go beyond the borders that so many people set for themselves.

But he hadn't wanted to.

She didn't get how he couldn't understand how much that hurt her. He framed their breakup as something caused entirely by her and her wanderlust, but he had promised her that he'd come too. As far as she was concerned, it was Ben who had broken his word.

Her eyes flitted to him, taking in his profile as he quietly read a book. He was tall, broad, and whipped into a fine shape that seemed to come from eating hearty, homecooked meals and doing labor-intensive work all day. His sandy-blond hair was a bit longer than he used to wear it, just slightly developing a curl to it. She remembered how shaggy it used to be in high school and how she would run her hands through it.

The truth was, she'd always had a bit of a thing for sandy-blond hair, and when the guy with almost that exact shade of hair at the school, who also happened to be handsome and popular, suddenly started talking to her, she had thought she was dreaming.

But it wasn't a dream. Just like how this wasn't a nightmare. No, this was her life now. Her awkward, uncomfortable, spiraling life.

There was only so much wallowing in her own misery that she could do, however, and so Chastity forced herself to take a deep breath. She should at least try to be an adult about things. After all, she was going back home in a month or so, provided her mother was all right, and Ben had been kind enough to give them a ride. He certainly didn't have to do that.

In truth, she almost wished he hadn't.

Getting up from her seat, she crossed to him and sat down. He lifted his head from his book but didn't quite turn his neck to look at her. Instead, he stared straight ahead at the wall—like he was afraid to look at her.

"Are you enjoying that?" she asked, having no idea how to start a conversation with the man that she had secretly been comparing all other men to since she was young.

"Enjoying what?" he asked, clearly surprised by the sudden conversation.

"The book."

"It's all right."

The corners of her mouth went up in a slight smile. It seemed that Ben still had his knack for short, simple answers. While he was a man of few words, when he did speak, it made people listen that much more.

"I read it about a year and a half ago, I think. I enjoyed it. I thought the writer had great imagery, and I'm a sucker for a bit of banter."

Now it was his turn to smile ever so slightly. "You always have been fairly silver-tongued."

"Oh, when you say it that way, it makes me sound a bit nefarious."

"Does it?" he replied innocently, his smirk increasing the tiniest bit more.

She turned, giving him one of her signature looks that she chronically employed at the diner where she worked between acting gigs. "If anyone is aware of the possible implications of their words, it's you."

"I have no idea what you mean," he said, impressively still holding his neutral tone. "I'm just a dumb cowboy after all."

Chastity almost snorted at that. "Anyone who thinks you're dumb is in for a rude awakening. I'd want to be there to see it when you totally cut the legs out from under them."

"Really? You think it'd be some sort of grand affair? I figured I would just talk to them if I wanted to prove them wrong."

Now she physically turned in her seat to look at him. It was so easy to slip into conversation with him, all their awkwardness from before fading to the background as the banter started to flow. "You like to pretend that you don't have a flair for the dramatic, but I know better than that."

He put the book down and glanced at her, his green eyes sharp and intense enough to make her heart skip a beat. "Oh, do you?"

She nodded, feeling excitement well up in her belly. "I can see it now. You'd play along, all taciturn and agreeable, until the perfect moment when you would suddenly reveal that you knew that they were trying to dupe you all along. There would be other people there too, so they could witness the realization as it swept across your victim's face."

"Uh-huh. And just who are these nefarious people whom I'm exposing?"

"Hey," she said, pointing a finger toward his face. "Don't go stealing my word."

"I'm pretty sure you didn't invent the word 'nefarious.'"

"How would you know? You're just a dumb cowboy."

Finally, his smirk grew into a full-blown smile. "I see. So, *you're* the bad guy." He leaned in ever so slightly, his warm breath ghosting over her face. Suddenly, she was keenly aware of just how...*there* he was. His broad shoulders, his calloused, tanned hands. All she needed to do was reach out and touch his—

No.

That was not good.

That was really not good.

Emotionally, she backpedaled and realized she was following a path that she couldn't be on. Swallowing hard, she said something she knew would stop whatever magnetism was pulling them together.

"That's how you've been painting me all these years, isn't it?"

She felt the hitch in his breath, and he sat back up. He didn't say a single word and instead picked up his book again.

Oh dear. Now Chastity felt guilty. She swore she didn't know if she was heads or tails with this man. All she knew was when she looked at him, it was so easy to feel like a young woman again, still fresh and free from all the bitterness handed to her while on the relentless treadmill of life. Back when anything was possible.

But that bubble was popped long ago. It would do her well

to remember that, lest she run into the same problems she always had.

She'd dated, sure, but of the three relationships she'd had since she left Blanche Creek, none of them had panned out. The first had been madly in love with her, but she couldn't feel the same way back. It was like her heart was somewhere else, outside of her body, and while she did enjoy his company, she never felt much else.

The second, she'd had more hope for, but then she found out he was hooking up with one of her friends. Apparently, he found her reluctance toward sex ridiculous, saying it was bizarre that she was nearly thirty and still a virgin.

It wasn't like she was so devoted to God that she'd taken a vow of *chastity*—*hah*, the irony of that. In fact, her faith had wavered multiple times in the city. It was just that she never felt close enough to anyone to do anything more intimate beyond kissing. It was like there was a level of trust that she couldn't reach.

Maybe she was broken.

"I'm sorry," she murmured, looking down at the ground. She could feel a wave of emotions coming on, and she was desperately trying to cut them off. She was strong and would get through this. She was letting the situation get to her far too much. "That was uncalled for."

"It's the truth," Ben said with a shrug. "For years you've been the girl who broke my heart, and I'd be lying if I said I didn't resent you for abandoning me."

"Abandoning *you*?" Chastity repeated. "You're the one who abandoned me."

"That's not how I remember it."

"Then you're remembering it *wrong*." It was a struggle to keep her voice calm, but somehow, she managed. "It happened in senior year after school between rehearsal breaks. You came to visit me, and we went outside to sit on the bleachers and complain about the director. You were wearing that blue turtleneck that I loved and had just cut your hair."

She closed her eyes, picturing it all.

"I can remember it like it was yesterday. I told you how I was going to go to Broadway and have my name in lights. I told you that I would prove to the director that I wasn't some chubby character actress and that I could be an ingénue.

"I remember distinctly that I paused and said I would work out some way to come visit you every month, Broadway or not, and you looked at me with those big, green eyes of yours, with all those lashes and starshine that comes with teenage love, and you said you would come with me."

Chastity tried to hold back the tears welling in her eyes.

"I don't know how you forgot that, because it's burned into my memory like the sun. I held your face in my hands, asking if you meant it, and you promised that you did. We kissed and kissed and kissed until I was dizzy, and then you tightly held my hand as we walked back inside."

Chastity could feel him staring at her, his mouth in a tight line for several moments. It took a lot of willpower to return his glance, and she was surprised to see guilt written across his features.

"I guess I had forgotten about that," he said, his voice almost too quiet to hear. "But I remember it now."

"How fortunate," she retorted less than gracefully. "Only twelve years later."

"I'm s—"

"Ms. Parker?"

Chastity's head snapped to the door to see a nurse standing

there. It was déjà vu from the other office, but she stood immediately. She had an idea of what was happening.

"Yes?"

"Your mother has requested that you meet with the doctor as her power of attorney."

"Right." Chastity looked to Ben, not wanting to leave things how they currently were, but not seeing much of a choice. "I'll be back."

She followed after the nurse, and once more was led into the back to an office.

A doctor was there, a tall woman with short blond hair and an intense expression. She smiled briefly when Chastity entered and gestured to a chair.

"Have a seat, please."

Chastity complied, and soon the doctor started talking.

"So Mrs. Parker requested that I talk to you because she was feeling confused. She gave me permission to explain the situation to you, is that okay?"

Chastity nodded. Was her mom having another one of her spells? Chastity hadn't really been around long enough to know if this was a thing of grief or the beginning of a long-term memory problem.

"Yes, please."

"Thank you." The doctor's face turned even more serious. "The earliest of our tests won't process until tomorrow, and several will take about four weeks to confirm any sort of diagnosis. But I do believe that your mother is displaying signs of dementia. It's too early to classify what kind it is—"

"There are multiple kinds of dementia?" Chastity interrupted, her heart squeezing in her chest.

Oh no.

This was it.

Her worst fears were coming true, and all she could do was sit and gawk at the doctor like she had grown another head.

Her father had just died, and she returned to her small hometown that felt anything but that. She just wanted to curl up and reconnect with the woman who raised her, smoothing over all of the rocky parts of their relationship until it was as healthy and supportive as it should be.

But even that was being taken away from her.

And even that was a selfish reaction. Her mother was sick, and all Chastity could think about was how it affected her. Since when had she become so narcissistic?

She didn't know, and she certainly wasn't getting the answer while staring at the doctor with her eyes half bulged out of her skull. Trying to calm herself, she took several deep breaths as the doctor explained.

"Yes, several. Dementia is more of a catch-all term. Like I said, it'll take about four weeks before we know everything for sure. So, what I'd like you to do is keep a journal of anything you notice that is unusual.

"This would include sudden moments of confusion, forgetting foundational memories, confusing the identities of people she's close with. Even if you think it's fairly innocuous, or not a big deal, I want you to write it down, as well as the time that it happened. That's vital."

"You're checking for sundowning syndrome," Chastity said, looking past her and off into the future.

She could almost see it all stretching out before her. The slow, inevitable decline of her mother, losing all the precious things that made her . . . her. Then Chastity really would be alone.

Why was God doing this? As far as Chastity knew, her mother was one of the most pious women in town. Why would he take away her husband, then her mind? It all seemed so cruel.

"I see you're informed. That will be useful."

Chastity nodded dully before taking a breath and pulling herself into the present. Medicine had come a long way since her friend's mother had passed five years earlier. Maybe that would help.

"Yes, I've tried to read up on it a bit. Is it okay if we go now?" she heard herself ask dully. But it was the only way she could keep her tone stable. She didn't want to break into hysterics or even emote her worry and agitate her mother once she sees her again. The woman had been through far too much lately.

"Yes. But before you go, have you considered an in-home aide? Honestly, it might end up being the best course of action over the coming months, all things considered."

"Aren't those... expensive?" Chastity wasn't sure how she was speaking around the lump in her throat, but somehow, she was managing.

"Depending on your insurance, they can be."

"I'll look into it. I guess I need to call the insurance people first."

"Yes, I think that would be best. There is a long road ahead of us, but there's no guarantee that this is an expiration date on your mother. I want you to remember that. Often people think that dementia is a death sentence, but there are some forms that are temporary, and reversible if treated appropriately."

"That's good to know. Is there anything else?"

"No, that should be about it. Please try to stay by the phone over the next few weeks. I'll put this as my priority."

"Thanks, I appreciate that."

And she really did.

True, the doctor was giving her some bad news, but at least

she was being polite about it and helping her as best she could. It wasn't like there was much else to do besides wait.

Walking through life like it was a strange dream, she followed the doctor to the room where her mom was waiting, crochet project half out of her bag but she was just staring at it like it was a foreign animal.

"Hey, Mom. Did you miss me?"

She looked up at Chastity and smiled, causing her heart to lurch. Would her mom recognize her, or would she think she was someone else today?

"There you are, dear," she said, putting her project away. "I was trying to finish that up, but for the life of me I couldn't remember what stitch I was using."

"It happens to everyone," Chastity said with a laugh, offering her mother her arm. Her mom, who Chastity now saw as more fragile, took it, and they headed out. Mrs. Parker went on a long tale about the skein of yarn that her husband had bought her two anniversaries ago. Chastity listened with a fake sort of smile, glad that her mom didn't seem to catch the tension beneath the surface.

They reached the waiting room, and Ben stood, sending her a look of concern. Chastity shook her head, and her mother continued to tell her tale to him. Thankfully, he seemed to catch her drift and didn't ask any questions, allowing her more time to think as they headed to the car.

It was only a bit past noon and yet already the day was incredibly stressful. She hoped that the tests would come back negative and that her mom would get back to normal.

She doubted it though.

11

Ben

*B*en helped Mrs. Parker into his truck, sparing another glance at Chastity. He wasn't sure what the news was, or why she was even here, but he could tell from Chastity's face that it wasn't good.

He may not be able to read her like he once could, but it was easy to see her brows knitted together and her dark eyes storming. He remembered she was like this once before, when her best friend had an ovarian cyst and had asked her not to tell anyone. She hated keeping secrets and seemed to internalize them into a heavy sort of responsibility.

He didn't like that she did that, and back then he had been the one to comfort her. But now he was...

No one.

The thought soured his mood, and he made sure Chastity got in before crossing over to his side.

It was a shame, really. During their conversation in the waiting room, it had almost felt like old times. It was far too easy to feel pulled to her, and after only a few lines of banter, he almost forgot about their bitter breakup that seemed to have left both of them scarred.

After all these years, he had been blaming everything on Chastity, but could it be that he was the one in the wrong? Had he blocked out those memories of his promise to ease his broken heart, or was it just an accident from too much time passing?

Who knew? Certainly not him. And all it took was another glance at Chastity's troubled face to realize there was even more going on that he wasn't privy too.

For the first part of the drive, Mrs. Parker kept the truck from being an uncomfortable silence by chatting away. She really was a lovely woman. It was a shame that she was possibly sick with something. Maybe that was what made her so confused earlier?

But after a while, she nodded off, resting her gray head against the cushioned head of the seat and breathing steadily. He was tempted to ask Chastity what was going on, but her full lips were pressed into a thin line and that told him that she wasn't in the mood for much talk.

And so the moments passed, with Ben not even willing to turn on the radio, lest he wake the woman. No doubt Mrs. Parker needed her sleep, even if it meant an hour or so of discomfort on his part.

Still, it seemed to be an eternity before he finally pulled up to the Parker's house. As he stopped the car, the woman beside him stayed sleeping, and Chastity looked from her mother to the front door of their house with concern.

"Don't worry," Ben said, reading the look on her face. "I'll get her for you."

She heaved a sigh of relief, and to Ben's surprise, it made him feel good. He needed to get home and clear his head before his emotions did anything else strange.

But first, he needed to help.

Throwing the car into park, he crossed around to Mrs. Parker's side and carefully opened the door. The woman didn't stir, even as he slid his muscled arms behind her back and under her legs.

Slowly, he pulled her to his chest until she was snugly in his grasp. The older woman was far too light for his tastes. He would have to see that his ma made her some fatty food to help her bulk up.

His eyes flitted to Chastity, who was looking to him with an apprehensive sort of gratitude. Against his better judgment, his gaze slid along her soft curves. As long as he could remember, both women had been beautifully feminine in their full-figured silhouettes, so feeling Mrs. Parker so slender was troubling.

"Lead the way," he said to Chastity, stepping to the side.

Of course, he knew his way around her old house. He had spent hours there after all. But the polite thing to do seemed to be to let her show him the way like they weren't familiar.

Yet even with those extra steps, déjà vu settled over him like a warm blanket. How many memories were made in the house he was stepping into? Hours studying, eating warm meals. Laughing and planning their future. While he had never been allowed in her room with the door closed, he could still recall perfectly what it looked like, as if they had just parted yesterday.

What was happening to him? He'd never been the sentimental type, and yet he felt like he was drowning in emotion. He didn't like it. It was cloying and stuck to the roof of his mouth like a bad taste. He wanted to go back to the ranch where everything made sense and where he wasn't feeling thrown into chaos by the beautiful woman that his heart ached for.

"I'll take her up to her room," he said, banishing those longing thoughts from his head and directing himself to the stairs.

It was all too easy to get her up the stairs, and then to her bed, where he gently set Chasity's fragile mother down. It seemed a bit strange to tuck Mrs. Parker in, but he didn't want to just leave her curled on top of her comforter. Sitting beside her, he offered a quick prayer for her health, or just a little lucidity. He knew that God had a plan for everything, but goodness, that path was plenty obscured at the moment. Surely, she and Chastity had been through enough already, hadn't they?

He didn't get an answer, but he knew that was how prayer worked, and he trusted God had a plan for them. Bidding the unconscious woman good night, he headed back downstairs.

Chastity was still standing at the foot of the stairs, her face toward the wall. At first Ben thought that perhaps she had been waiting for him, but then he noticed that her gaze was affixed to the many portraits that lined the staircase.

Ben remembered several of the moments depicted. When Chastity had won Battle of the Books, and when she had been cast as the lead in the school play. When her father had been promoted at work. When they had gone to the high school prom.

So many happy memories, yet they seemed so melancholy. Like dozens of slices of everything she was losing instead of treasured snapshots of a life well-lived.

Ben wasn't quite sure what to do, so he cleared his throat

before speaking. "Hey, are you okay?"

She didn't budge at first, and for a moment, he thought she hadn't heard him. But then her head slowly turned toward him, as if she was made of stone and had just come to life.

Those eyes.

Once more he was caught up in those swirling pools of almost-black eyes. Bottomless and filled with swirling emotion, he felt like her gaze was swallowing him whole. Pain, worry, concern, all of it whirled in that expression, stealing his breath away.

"Chastity..."

He wasn't sure what he was going to say, but apparently that simple word was all that she needed. Suddenly, she was closing the space between them until her arms were around him and her head was against his chest.

He stiffened for a moment, surprised, but softened after a breath. Bending slightly, he wrapped his arms around her as well, holding her as she sobbed against his chest.

It pained him to hear her hurting so terribly. He wanted her to be happy, even if he resented her for leaving him. But then again, hadn't he found out that *he* was the one who had broken his promise to her? Did that mean that he was the one in the wrong all these years?

Perhaps. But it didn't really matter. The only thing that was important was the woman sobbing in his arms and the connection he could feel tying her to him.

He stroked her dark hair, slowly rocking her a bit. How many times had he wished to run his fingers through the black strands again? Too many to count. She had always been a bit vain about her long tresses, and he couldn't quite blame her.

While Chastity and her mother had never lived on the reservation, their Native American features were still distinct.

She had taught him the value her culture placed on their hair, even if she and her mother were only part Native, and many other things that he might not have heard of otherwise. It wasn't like they were actually taught about Native American culture in school.

The minutes passed, punctuated by her tears and sobs, but he let her take as much time as she needed. He felt as if he could hold her forever. Her fortress in the storm. Someone that she could cling to in the whirlwind that she was swept up in.

"Honey! Honey, where are you?"

Mrs. Parker's frantic voice cut through the moment, and Chastity shuttered, pulling her soft, warm body away from Ben. He wanted to reach out and continue to hold her to his side, but he refrained.

"Sorry," she said faintly, wiping the tears from her face. He wanted to tell her that she had nothing to apologize for at all, but then she was clearing her throat and turning away. "I better go check on her. Thank you. For... everything, I guess."

"It was nothing. Really."

She looked like she wanted to say something more, but then her mother called out again, and she hurried up the stairs, then out of sight.

Ben stood there for several moments, blinking and trying to order his thoughts. He felt like he was torn somewhere between the teenage him that had been so foolhardily in love and his grown self, who didn't have time for silly relationship shenanigans or gold diggers.

Somehow his feet led him toward the door, and he wandered out to his truck, where he got in. Mind whirling, he turned the engine on and headed home.

He wasn't sure what was happening, but the twisting in the pit of his stomach told him that it wasn't anything good.

12

Chastity

*T*he wind kicked up, throwing the fine dirt of the small town into Chastity's face as she walked down the street. It did nothing to improve her mood, which was already quite sour.

But didn't she have enough reason to feel sour? Lately, it seemed like she was busy either shoving away emotions she didn't want to deal with or drowning in stress and fear. It wasn't a pleasant sort of sensation, but she didn't see a way out.

It had been a week since that fateful doctor's appointment, and she'd been waiting by the phone and with her cell on full volume the entire time. Most of the days her mother seemed perfectly fine—aside from grieving the love of her life. But sometimes it was very clear that something was wrong with her. Either she would talk like a child, or mistake Chastity for a friend, or wonder when her dead husband was getting back.

Chastity made sure to write it down dutifully in the journal she was using, but she was filling up the pages far too quickly for her liking.

It was those reasons that she was loath to leave her mother alone, but she had realized that she had to. Her cell phone bill was coming up, and they were almost out of meals that people had given them at her father's funeral. Chastity had assumed that her mother was a bit more financially set in her older years, but a quick look into her parents' checking account had told her that it was almost empty.

She hadn't meant to snoop, but the gas bill had come in, and her mother had asked her to take care of it since it used to be Chastity's dad's job and her mother just couldn't bring herself to do it. Naturally, Chastity had agreed, but she hadn't expected to be faced with the fact that both she *and* her mother were very, *very* broke.

Actually, it was worse than that.

Her parents had been in debt.

The gas bill was the only thing that was current. But their electric and mortgage were both two months behind. Why had they let it get so bad? Why hadn't they told Chastity? She wasn't sure what she would have done if they had told her, but she would have done *something*. She would have fought tooth and nail to make sure it didn't get to that point.

And so, it was while lying in bed, realizing that she was stuck in town for another three weeks at minimum, that she knew she had to get a job.

Easier said than done.

Unlike the city, where she could just hop on the internet and see what was available, she had to visit all the shops in town in person with a resume in hand. It was like living in the

Stone Age, and she put a check in the column for one of the bad things about living in a small town.

She'd visited the bookstore, the library, the clinic, and the only fast food joint in town yesterday and was now on her way to the local grocery store. Although it had started off as a Ma-and-Pa shop when her mother was a kid, it had expanded into an almost castle-like building—complete with a clocktower that dwarfed everything except the church in town.

As Chastity strode up to the building, she saw it was just like she remembered. Stopping in front of the glass doors, she made sure to straighten herself up before heading in.

Being a weekday during the school year, there weren't a whole lot of people milling around. Chastity managed to spot a cashier, who was waiting on the only customer in his line.

She strode over and waited until he was done. Something about his face rang a bell in the back of her mind. She couldn't quite place it, however, so she kept the nostalgia to herself as she greeted him.

"Hey there," she said with a broad smile. "Do you know if you guys are hiring at all?"

The cashier looked to her, and his hazel eyes grew wide in disbelief. "Are you kidding me? Chastity Parker is that you?"

Chastity blinked at him, a bit shocked by his amazed tone. She still had no idea who he was and that was quickly growing embarrassing. "Uh... yes?"

"Dude, I haven't seen you in *years*." She must have still been staring at him in bewilderment because he laughed heartily and explained himself. "I don't expect you to remember me. I was just some dumb underclassman and an understudy in our school's play when you were a senior. But man, I had the *biggest* crush on you. When I heard that you'd left town for college, I was devastated."

He laughed again and offered his hand. "Jeremy Comstock," he said with a grin. "Nice to finally introduce myself. So, what brings you back home?"

"My father died."

His jovial expression dimmed a bit. "Oh, my goodness, I'm so sorry. I think I read about that in the paper. I just didn't connect the dots that *that* Mr. Parker was your father. Are you all right?"

Well, if the cat was already out of the bag, why not be completely honest? "Actually, not really." She took a deep breath. Normally, she was not this open. One of the complaints her few partners had was that she never opened up, so telling such intimate details to a stranger was wholly bizarre. "Turns out my parents' finances weren't exactly in order. My mom is in pretty bad shape now, so I was hoping to get a job while I figure things out."

"Geez, yeah, that's rough." He shook his head, and to her dismay, his expression didn't brighten to offer her a job or give her advice about how to get one. In fact, the next words out of his mouth were quite the opposite. "Man, if you're looking here, I don't think you're gonna have a good time of it."

Chastity's stomach squeezed. "What do you mean?"

"Well, do you remember the owners? They're super staunch about supporting the town and usually only hire people they've known for ages. No offense, but when you left for the Big Apple, everyone figured you thought the town wasn't good enough for you. You can try, but I don't think it's likely that they'll be interested in hiring you."

"Oh."

What could she say to that? That was years ago. Certainly, they wouldn't hold a teenager's enthusiasm for escaping her hometown against her, would they?

Jeremy must have seen her crestfallen expression because he scrambled to cheer her up. "But who knows? Maybe I'm wrong. I'll talk to the owner and see if I can put in a good word for you. I think he was friends with your pops, so that certainly can't hurt."

"Thank you," Chastity said softly, feeling like she was caught between gratitude and anger. Too much of her current situation wasn't fair. "I would really appreciate it."

"No problem. That's what friends are for, right? Or in this case, underclassmen who you never knew existed in high school."

"Yeah, you're so funny," she tried to joke. "Well, I'm going to head out. Here's my resume if he bends at all." She handed over the paper as calmly as she could before leaving, but once she was on the street, all of her emotions were threatening to well out of her.

It just wasn't fair! She was a hard worker. And she would make sure that she did her best. Why would anyone hold the fact that she had escaped from the tiny town against her? Didn't any of them ever want to spread their wings and live somewhere else? Where their destiny wasn't already decided for them from the day they were born?

Ugh.

It wouldn't help her employment chances to have a temper tantrum in the street, so she headed home. Maybe she could go on a run later at the high school. Students were rarely there after it got dark, and it was nice to jog around the track under the starlight.

Or at least that was what she had done back in high school. While she had never been very fast—thick thighs always protesting if too much friction happened—she had enjoyed the endorphins. It also helped that Ben had often driven there to meet her. She could still feel how her heart rate would speed up at the site of him. Occasionally there were kisses and cuddles, but mostly he just watched to make sure she was safe from coyotes and stray ranch hands.

No, she didn't need to think about those nights right now. Ever since the last time she had seen Ben, she had done her best to keep him solidly out of her mind. It was clear that, in her emotional state, she was getting confused from being around him, which was ridiculous. They weren't in love. Not anymore. In fact, they were probably in hate. So, the best thing to do would be to forget that he existed. He seemed to have forgotten her just fine since the appointment at the doctor's office.

Chastity kicked a rock, muttering to herself as she headed home. It didn't take her long, but as she cut through a yard and saw the porch looming into view, she realized someone was standing there.

Her pace picked up, and she could see her mother standing in the doorway, hands on her hips and face flushed. The person on the porch was a man in a suit, and he towered over her mom's frail form.

Chastity could tell by both of their body language that it wasn't a pleasant conversation, and she sped toward them. As she got closer, she could hear her mother's raised voice insisting that he leave. That was enough for her, and she cleared her throat.

"Excuse me," she said, moving past him on the porch to insert herself between him and her mother. "Do you have business here?"

The man was a strange one, she realized now that she was standing close to him. His features were pleasant enough, but there was a cold sort of deadness behind his eyes and a viper's kiss to his smile. He looked both stiff and sleezy at the same time, something Chastity hadn't thought was possible until that moment. His light, blond hair was slicked back like a helmet, and his blue eyes were downright frigid.

"Yes, with Mrs. Parker. I work with several financial institutions and need to speak with her directly."

Financial institutions? Crap.

"Well, I'm Ms. Parker and her power of attorney. My mother is under a great deal of stress right now, so you can direct any questions you have to me."

"Is that so? How convenient for you to show up when you did then." He set his briefcase down on the rail and pulled out a manila envelope, which he handed over to Chastity. "I work for First Stone Bank, and we have helped your parents manage their debt in the hopes to pay it off with less interest. However, after the passing of the account holder, I'm afraid that our previous arrangement is no longer in effect. We would like to work something out with Mrs. Parker and open an account in her name. However, her nearly non-existent credit history prevents us from giving her the same variables Mr. Parker had."

Chastity felt her cheeks burn as her temper whipped up. Because, of course, this had to happen now. "Really? My father died less than a month ago and you've come to badger my mom about money?"

"I give my condolences and realize that this is, indeed, a difficult time. But it is imperative that we get ahead of this so that their debt doesn't balloon with late fees and other penalties."

Chastity sighed. At least this guy was polite. Sure, his timing was a bit cruel and he looked like he was dipped in sleaze and rolled around in a crumble of underhanded, but he was just doing his job.

"Look, my mother is ill—"

"What? No, I'm not! I'm just mad that this suit from some city came onto my porch, badgering me about your father's affairs."

His tone turned sharp as he addressed her mother over her shoulder. "For the last time, Mrs. Parker, I apologize for the poor timing, but it is just one of the things—"

"This isn't necessary," Chastity cut in. "Let's step away, shall we? Like I said, my mother isn't exactly herself—"

"Not myself? He's a dirty scoundrel!" That made Chastity's head whip in her direction. In all her years of life, she had never heard her mother talk to anyone that way. And sure, it was pretty low on the filthy-mouth totem pole, but it was still bizarre to hear. "And stop treating me like a child."

"*Please*," Chastity repeated at the man, feeling what little patience she had slip. "Let's talk a bit away, okay?"

But he stood there like a rock, his bright eyes boring into Mrs. Parker. "I am here to help you. I would appreciate if you treated me with the same respect you would give any professional."

"I'll show you respect, you—"

"*Sir!*" For the second time in a few moments, Chastity found herself interrupting a string of expletives from her mother. When all of this was over, she needed to remember to put this in her mother's health journal, because she was pretty sure that late afternoon or evening aggression was a sign of sundowning. "Please!"

She placed her hand on his arm, internally pleading with him to stop engaging with her mother and go deal with things far enough away to be productive. But instead of budging, his hand covered hers.

"Your mother is quite rude," he sneered, his expression

darkening. "Tell me, are you more polite than the woman who raised you?"

"I *told* you, she's ill. She's not normally like this."

"What she is normally like doesn't so much matter as what she is *now*." His fingers curled around hers, and she suddenly found herself unable to pull away. "Honestly, I'm liable to go to the bank and tell them just how inhospitable she is. Unless... you were able to convince me otherwise."

Chastity stared at him with wide eyes, wondering if she was hearing what she thought she was hearing. "Pardon me?"

His fingers tightened, pinching into her tanned skin. "I am a forgiving man. I can think of one, or perhaps two things that might motivate me to forget that my conversation with Mrs. Parker even happened."

Oh.

Oh *no*.

He was saying exactly what Chastity feared he meant, and all she could do was stare at him in shock. He wanted her to sleep with him?

This couldn't be real. People didn't do this in small towns like this, did they?

He took a step toward her, closing the gap between them, and suddenly Chastity found herself faced with a decision that she never thought she would come across. Part of her wanted to haul off and punch him with all of her might, but another, very small and scared part of her was wondering what all the consequences were if she were to say no.

"Well, Ms. Parker?"

13

Ben

*B*en watched as water poured over his hands, some of it splashing up over the side of the small bathroom sink as he wondered just how he had ended up back at the Parker house.

It was borderline pathetic really. It had been a week since he had last seen Chastity, and he couldn't get her out of his head. She ran through his thoughts on a nearly hourly basis, anything and everything reminding him of her. From the faint scent of vanilla from his mother baking cookies, to her favorite morning glories blooming with the sunrise, even to the way his horse Gertie would wuffle for treats. Goodness knows how much Chastity had spoiled his last mount with carrots, sugar cubes, and apples.

So, after several nights of unsatisfied sleep and roaming thoughts, he had convinced himself to visit—if only to check on

Mrs. Parker and deliver some fatty foods that he had asked Ma to make if she had the free time.

Of course, Ma was pleased as punch that he was heading over there. He had the feeling that her heart had never closed to the idea of him and Chastity being together, even though Ben had told himself for years that he would never be with her again. She had always referred to the young woman as her future daughter-in-law and had been quite upset when they had broken up. Ben wanted to tell her that nothing was happening between them now, but he hadn't. Instead, he took the warm, packaged-up meals from her and hopped in his truck.

But when he arrived, straightening his plaid shirt before picking up the food and knocking on the door, he soon found out that Chastity was out for an hour or two.

For a moment, Ben had figured that it was a sign and he should let sleeping dogs lie, but then his mouth had been moving and he offered to make some tea for the smiling Mrs. Parker. Naturally, she happily accepted, and he crossed over to the fridge to put the food away.

He didn't like the sight he had been greeted by. The fridge was practically empty, with only half of a casserole and some condiments in the door. Turning back to Mrs. Parker, he had asked if they were running short.

She seemed much more lucid than at her trip to the doctor's office, and she happily explained that Chastity was out buying groceries. Apparently, they'd been so busy that they had completely forgotten about them until they had run out a few days ago. Ben wasn't sure how much he believed that, but he didn't want to argue the point and instead went about making tea.

"What am I even doing here?" Ben asked himself, squirting

some of the soap into his hands and lathering up. He made sure to get under his nails where dirt and grime from working liked to stick. While he didn't mind getting filthy for his work, his mother had drilled into him how important it was to have clean hands in front of company.

But his mind was already back to retracing his steps. They had been sitting down at the table, chitchatting about the old times. She seemed to remember all of them and who he was. It really seemed as if she was an entirely different woman from the one he had taken to the doctor.

Eventually, however, the tea grew cold in his third cup and he had excused himself to the bathroom. Now he found himself staring at the mirror with water still pouring over his hands.

Yelling sounded from down on the first floor, and Ben quickly turned off the faucet, wiping his hands on one of the neat towels hanging from a rack. The shouting only increased as he struggled with the bathroom door for a moment. It had a habit of sticking back when he and Chastity were in high school, and apparently, it was still just as stubborn.

When he was finally out and down the stairs, he could hear Mrs. Parker rattling off an obscene string of swear words and a man answering her. He strode for the entrance, completely baffled, and words started to reach him.

"Unless... you were able to convince me otherwise." That was the unknown male voice. Ben knew instantly that he didn't like the sounds of that. It was somewhere between oil and ice, with little pricks of calculation in it.

"Pardon me?" That was Chastity. He knew her voice in an instant. She sounded completely surprised, which made him wonder what exactly the man was asking her to convince him of.

Ben was almost to the door when he got the answer. "I am a

forgiving man. I can think of one, or perhaps two things that might motivate me to forget that my conversation with Mrs. Parker even happened." There was a beat of silence, and Ben realized exactly what he was asking. His cheeks burned red, and suddenly the entire world shrank down as his anger swelled up inside of him. "Well, Ms. Parker?"

He could hear Chastity stammering something, but that was all she managed to get out before he was out the door. He crossed the distance, spotting the man's hand wrapped around Chastity, and he ripped it from her.

"Can I help you?" he said, iron to his voice.

He took in every feature that he could about the man, unwilling to forget what he looked like. While Ben was not a violent man, he could feel rage seething below his skin, urging him to throttle the guy right in the nose.

"I don't know who you are, sir, but I am here on business with the Parkers. Unhand me, now, before I feel the need to get the authorities involved."

"Authorities?" Ben spat. The gall of this man. He knew this type; he was a city slicker, so drunk on power and greed that he thought he could order people this way and that while he gloated from his lofty position. "I'm sure they would be interested in the fact that you were propositioning a customer. You know soliciting sexual services is illegal here, no matter how big your pocket books are."

"I recognize that your hillbilly pride no doubt compels you to solve everything with your fist, but I assure you that is not the wisest course of action."

Ben took a step closer, still gripping the man's hand. "If I wanted to strike you, I would. Now I suggest you get off this property before I lose my restraint."

"How typical. It seems that you and Mrs. Parker are cut

from the same cloth. So much for Western kindness. We'll see how well your proclivity for vulgarity will do when calculating her new repayment—"

He never finished his sentence, but that was probably because a fist struck him right across the face, sending his head whipping to the side. Ben let go, staring in wonder as Chastity threw yet another punch that hit him in the chest.

"How *dare* you!" she cried, her eyes blazing with a righteous anger that Ben hadn't seen since she was a freshman fending off a school bully. "You come to my home, you agitate my mother then insult her, you talk to me as if I'm some sort of prostitute, then you have the *audacity* to threaten my mother's livelihood!"

The man righted himself and looked at Chastity with complete and utter surprise. While Ben was astounded too, he at least had seen her like this once before. A whirling tempest of a woman, a force of nature, staring him down like some sort of mighty, ancient deity from myth.

"You punched me!"

"You bet I did!" she snapped. "And I'll do it again if you don't go back to your bank in the city and work out a deal that will help my mother. I don't want your charity, but you fight as hard as you can to get her a similar arrangement like you gave my father, and I won't file a report that you tried to solicit sexual services from me. You got that?"

"You're in no position to order me—"

Chastity lunged toward him, and Ben quickly strode forward and caught her, his strong arms wrapping around her middle. For a moment, he allowed himself to enjoy the feeling of her form against his once more, but he quickly shoved it out of his head. Now was not the time.

"If you think First Stone Bank is—"

Now it was Ben's turn to interrupt. He would almost feel bad that the man hadn't been able to finish a sentence in minutes, but he was far too much of a sleaze ball. "Wait, did you say First Stone Bank?"

The man straightened himself and looked surprised by the question. "Yes. What of it?"

"Oh, my family has several accounts with them. Perhaps you know of us. Does the name Miller sound familiar to you?"

All the color drained from his face, and he looked to Ben with wide eyes, completely ignoring how Chastity was still straining against him to possibly rip the man's face off.

"Millers as in, uh, the Miller Ranch?"

"Yeah. Exactly," Ben said, feeling the dynamic shift. "I'm Benedict Miller, to be exact. The eldest son. But if this is how your bank treats its patrons, I think it might be time to move our accounts elsewhere."

"Now wait a minute. I—I see there has been a misunderstanding. Ms. Parker, I will make sure they are convinced to reinstate your father's arrangement. We want to make everything as comfortable for you as we can in this time of need. Please, don't hesitate to call."

"Thank you," Ben said, barely withholding his smirk.

The man picked up his briefcase, which he dropped before picking it up again, and rushed off, leaving Ben still holding Chastity.

"Are you going to let me go?" Chastity asked after another moment.

"Oh. Right."

Ben reluctantly released his hold on her, and they both turned to the door only to see Mrs. Parker standing there breathlessly, her hands on her hips.

"Now what in the good Lord's name was that?" she said sternly, reminding Ben of the time she had caught him and

Chastity making out on her bed. "I know that man wasn't right with God, but that's no excuse for violence. Chastity. When did I teach you to use your fists instead of your words?"

"Sorry, Mom," Chastity said, calming down from her previous furor. Ben was surprised that she didn't argue further, but a quick glance in her direction showed that she looked both embarrassed and tired. He wondered if her shopping trip had been especially stressful for her.

"Well, I suppose it can't be helped. I—I think I might have used some language I shouldn't. I..." Suddenly the imposing woman wilted a bit. "I'm awfully tired. I think I should go lie down. Will you two be all right?"

"We'll be fine, ma'am," Ben said quickly. Judging by the woman's pale face and red cheeks, she looked like she should indeed go lie down.

"Please, call me Auntie Parker, like you used to."

Ben nodded, and she wandered back into the house, leaving only Chastity and him on the front walkway.

"I can't believe that just happened," Chastity groaned, holding her head in her hands.

"I can't believe you just punched a guy."

"I can't believe I *only* punched that guy," she said with a smirk. "He deserved a lot worse."

"Yeah, and if I wasn't here, you might have given it to him."

"You bet I would have."

They both shared a laugh, the stress of the situation fading away. Suddenly, all the walls were dropped, and Ben found himself unable to deny how amazingly attracted he was to this woman—whether she was pensively looking out of a window, her dark eyes swirling with concern, or whether she was punching a man in the face, rage radiating from her like a legendary fury.

From the moment their eyes had locked in that funeral home, he'd been caught up in the wonder that was Chastity Parker all over again. He was like a fly in a web, but there wasn't anywhere else he wanted to be.

"Hey Chastity," he murmured. She turned her head, and once more he was swallowed up by those perfect, onyx eyes.

"Yeah?"

His heart thundered in his chest, and his blood seemed to rush too loudly in his veins. Part of him, the one that had spent the past ten years shutting himself from the rest of the world and his heartache, told him to keep his mouth shut and go home before he made the same mistake he had made as a teenager. But there was another part of him, the one that he had tried to keep shut away for all these years that urged him onward.

"Wanna go on a date?"

14

Chastity

*C*hastity brushed her hair up into a tight ponytail, regarding the mirror as she wrangled her long tresses into a sleek but hopefully effortless-looking shape. Her makeup was done, complete with pouty dark lips and eyeshadow, and her outfit was spread out on her bed. She was practically ready, if only her hair would just cooperate.

Wanna go on a date?

Ben's words echoed through her mind, and she looked to her reflection conspiratorially. She knew that nothing good could come from this idea, and yet—for some reason—she had agreed.

It wasn't like anyone could blame her. The way he had come barreling out of the house, ripping that man's hands away from her had reminded her about everything that had first made her fall in love with him. His kindness, his morals, the way he had always tried to protect her, but never treated her as if she was weak herself. He was like a knight in shining armor, but one who also handed her a sword when she needed one.

And, more importantly, took that sword away when she didn't need it.

She really would have beaten that guy into next Sunday if Ben hadn't stopped her. And for that, she was immensely grateful. Also, him dropping his family name had completely turned the situation around. Chastity had never been one to use the Miller wealth or prestige for herself, but for once, she was glad for the unforeseen ace up her sleeve.

"I'm crazy, aren't I?" she asked her reflection, still wrangling some baby hairs that were refusing to cooperate. "This is the man I left ten years ago after he broke a promise to me. I swore to myself I would never look back, and yet, here I am."

Not surprisingly, her reflection didn't have an answer for her. It just mirrored the furrow in her brow and the uncertainty flashing through her eyes. Was this stupid? It had to be stupid, right?

Yet, as stupid as it might be, she couldn't help but feel excited about it. When Ben was holding her in his arms again, his warm chest and abs pressed against her back, she was instantly drenched in all of those old feelings she used to have for him. Even after a decade, he still made her heart skip and her belly flip like a trapeze act.

Finally, her hair cooperated, and she went to change. After Ben had uttered that fateful sentence, asking if she wanted to go on a date with him, she had stared at him for a good minute before her English finally came back to her. Thankfully, she was able to keep some of her wits about her and asked him where it would be while her mind tried to catch up on whether she wanted to say yes or no.

That was when he suggested a nice place on his land. Normally, Chastity would insist on neutral locations for meetups, but this was Ben. She knew him and his family and trusted them implicitly with her safety.

Just maybe not with her heart.

Her alarm went off, signaling an hour until Ben arrived. Once more, she found herself questioning why she was doing this. She and Ben had broken up for a reason. There was no need to rehash all of that again.

And yet her heart was thundering, as if it was their first date all over again. She remembered the first time he had asked her out, shoulders broad, and hair flopping over in the way that was popular at the time. Even though they had become friends, she had stared at him like he had declared he was an alien from another planet. And honestly, that would have been plausible to the teenage version of herself.

She had been chubby, didn't use makeup, and kept her hair in a permanent bun. She was awkward anywhere but on stage, and she loved books and plays more than most people. So naturally, when one of the most handsome guys in school—who just so happened to be incredibly rich and sought after— showed interest in her, she assumed it was some sort of joke.

But it hadn't been. And thus, had started a three-year relationship that ended dramatically, as teen relationships were wont to do. But she had loved him. The head-over-heels, can't-breathe-without-you kind of love. And he had broken her heart.

So why was she going back in?

She could keep asking herself that question as many times as she liked, but she wouldn't have an answer anytime soon. Instead, she busied herself with looking over her outfit one more time before traveling into the hall.

"Oh, my goodness, you look lovely."

Her mother's voice drew her eyes up from the cute flats that she was wearing. Part of her had wanted to wear heels, but she knew better than to do so on a date with Ben.

"Thank you, Mom," Chastity said, giving her mother a small smile. When was the last time Mrs. Parker had seen her all dressed up? Even before she started skipping out on holidays, she still preferred to lounge around in sweats and loose clothing. Had the last time been... prom? Goodness, that was long ago.

"This brings me back, it does. It really does. If only Charles —" she cut herself off, her eyes watering. "Well, let's not think about that, shall we? Just look at my little girl, my beautiful, gorgeous little girl."

She held out her arms, and Chastity walked into them, giving her a warm hug. Funny, she had spent so much time running away from home, trying to never look back, and now she was feeling guilty for having missed so much. Was this what growing up was like?

Eventually they parted, then headed down the stairs to wait. Her mother put some tea on, and they reminisced about the old times. It seemed like she did that often. It probably wasn't healthy to spend so much time in the past, but she had far too much on her mind to worry about that now.

As the clocked ticked down to Ben's arrival, Chastity caught her mother staring at her several times. Fearing another episode, the young woman cleared her throat.

"Are you okay, Mom?"

She nodded, her voice warbling again. "Just hoping that one day I'll get to see you in a wedding dress."

Chastity felt herself color. What a thing to mention before a date. "I wouldn't count on me ever doing that."

Her brows furrowed ever so slightly. "Why ever not?"

"Romance isn't for me."

"Nonsense! You and Ben used to be quite a pair. I still remember the way you two used to look at each other, even after all these years. You can't love like that and then shut it off for the rest of your life."

"Can't I?" Chastity answered noncommittedly. Her mother opened her mouth to continue, and Chastity sighed. "Could we please change the subject? This is making me so uncomfortable I'm thinking about canceling the date altogether."

"All right then, I'll mind my business." But still, that knowing, motherly smile was on her face, and it drove Chastity mad. She knew that this date was a bad idea. She should have never agreed to it.

"Don't forget that you're getting a visit from one of the nurses today. She'll be here in about half an hour."

It had been hard convincing her mother that there was a need for medical personnel in the house at all, and even harder to convince her insurance, but with the help of the town doctor and the one in the city, she'd gotten them to agree to send a night nurse twice a week for four hours. It wasn't a ton, obviously, but it was enough to allow Chastity her moments of freedom and to get out of the house. Thankfully, her mom's episodes had leveled off and didn't seem to be escalating. Unfortunately, the fact that her mom had called her so many different people's names lately kept Chastity from feeling totally at ease.

There was the sound of a car pulling up, and then Chastity's phone went off. She checked it and saw the text she had been waiting for.

He was here.

"I'll be back home later tonight," Chastity said, hopping to her feet and giving her mother a kiss on the cheek. "Don't wait up for me. The nurse will be here soon, so try to be nice. You have my number if you need anything, anything at all."

But her mom didn't seem even remotely concerned about the new nurse she was getting. "You know, you're old enough where you could stay out all night if you so wished."

"*Mother*," Chastity reprimanded. "That doesn't sound like something a godly woman would do."

But she just shrugged, giving a mischievous look. "I'll pray for his forgiveness if you make me a godly grandmother."

Chastity sputtered a laugh and ducked out the door before her mother could get anymore brilliant ideas. Goodness, something had gotten into her, and Chastity wasn't sure if it was her illness or that strange way all mothers got when they wanted their progeny to pump out their own offspring.

But thankfully, she was suddenly out on the porch, the twilight sky dripping from golden honey into the soft velvet kiss of night. There, in front of their house, stood Ben's now-familiar silver pick-up. How she hadn't noticed it when the bank man had been visiting was beyond her, but that didn't matter now.

Chastity looked down at her black slacks with the lace detailing on the sides and her loose, floral top. It was simple, but she didn't want to wear a dress or skirt on the ranch. She had learned that lesson when she was younger and got saddle-rash on her thighs.

She walked up to the truck, but before she could get there, Ben was out of the car and walking around to open the door for her. Ever the gentleman, he was. She remembered always admiring that about him. Some guys did it to be showy, or to prove how amazing they were, but it wasn't like that with Ben. He seemed to do it as a matter of course and didn't expect any praise for it. Chastity knew a lot of men who could learn from him.

"Thank you," she said, getting in and taking the hand he offered her. Once more, it was like electricity shot through her, filling her with a rushing warmth that was full of so much hope and promise. She had spent all these years thinking that it was the big city that was cold, but maybe it was just her.

No, that was too ridiculous.

Wasn't it?

Such introspective thoughts were going to ruin her light-hearted mood worse than her mother, so she cut them off. Thankfully, Ben was already in on the other side and starting his truck up.

"So, where is your silver steed taking us?"

"The ranch," he answered.

"Well yeah, you said as much when you first asked me out. But the Miller Ranch is *huge*. I was more curious as to where we were going on your land."

He smiled at her, and Chastity could see a streak of the mischievous boy he had been. "You'll see."

Chastity sighed and shook her head. She couldn't resist smiling even though he was frustrating her.

He laughed, and just like that, she was totally relaxed. Apparently, being with Ben was like riding a bike once she stopped fighting it and telling herself she couldn't.

On the way to the ranch, Chastity asked about his family and what each of his brothers was up to. After what seemed like no time at all, they passed the front gates of his family's ranch. It was crazy to think that it had been there for hundreds of years, first founded by the Millers before Montana was even a state. It was just one big area of the country that was in unorganized territory back then.

They pulled off of the main road and hit a light set of tire tracks that stretched across the green field. Chastity vaguely recalled going this way once but couldn't remember where it led.

That didn't matter though, because she was feeling a long-lost sort of contentment. Something about the green grass, the fresh breeze, and the slight whiff of livestock in the air made her feel secure. Like nothing bad could ever happen to her here.

Except that wasn't quite true, was it? There was a very specific spot, under a tree and by one of the ponds where he had broken her heart. It had been a long walk back home from that particular fallout, and she wasn't interested in repeating it.

But certainly, that wouldn't happen today. After all, this was only a simple date. A nice hang out between two adults. Nothing expected of them, and certainly no relationship.

And honestly, the lack of pressure was nice. It was what it was. She could feel whatever she felt without her mind coming in and complicating everything.

Finally, a familiar building loomed over a gentle hill, and Chastity recognized it, letting out a slight gasp.

"The horses?" she whispered, hardly daring to believe it.

But she knew those lavender walls and the dark blue shutters. They had been painted that way by Ben's great-great-great-grandfather, who had wanted to impress the local school-teacher by painting it her favorite colors. Apparently, it had worked, because she ended up being Ben's great-great-great-grandmother.

"You remember," he said, that crooked smile growing a bit.

"Did you think I could forget? This was where we went on our first date on your ranch. I met... oh what was your horse's name at the time? Greta? No, Genevieve! She almost bit my hand off when I first gave her an apple."

"And then she didn't, and you proceeded to spoil her until

—" he cut himself off, frowning, but Chastity knew what he had been going to say.

"Until I left," Chastity finished for him. She didn't see any reason in beating around the bush. Was their past uncomfortable, dramatic, and full of heartbreak? Yeah. But it was how they had gotten to this point and ignoring that just seemed silly.

"Yeah. Until you left."

A quiet settled over the truck, as they pulled up to the barn. However, it wasn't out of awkwardness, or discomfort, but rather because Chastity was caught up in all the nostalgia of everything that she was seeing and feeling.

Hay tickled at her nose, and she could almost hear the idle wuffling of the many horses inside. While the Miller family didn't raise horses for shows or pageants, every one of them had their own mount, and they would often raise and train them as gifts for their workers or extended family members. Chastity remembered that Ben had once promised her one as a wedding gift.

It was a shame that was never going to happen now.

But she tucked those thoughts out of her head and hopped out of the truck as soon as it stopped. Happy that she was wearing flats with a good sole, she marched right up to the barn.

This was going to be a good night indeed.

15

Ben

Ben watched perhaps a little too keenly as Chastity marched right up to the barn, looking far more excited than he had ever hoped she would be. Part of him had been worried that she would resent the horses and the memories that they were tied to, but the smile that had burst from her face when she saw the building had been borderline intoxicating.

She was oblivious to the paralyzing effect she had on him, however, and her eyes were glued to the building all the way until he pulled up and parked.

Shaking his head to himself, he slid out of his truck and went to open the door for her.

She was bouncing from foot to foot, and he tried not to pay attention to the alluring movements of her body. He always felt like he was balancing somewhere between appreciating all the facets of her beauty and thinking thoughts that he certainly wouldn't want his mother or the reverend to hear. He remembered when he was young, he'd barely resisted temptation several times, and it was only Chastity's determination not to be another teenage statistic that had kept the boundaries so solid between them.

As he opened the door for her, he had a quick flicker of curiosity if those same boundaries held now that she was an adult. Had she found a lover in the city who had touched her the way his teenage self had always longed to? It certainly wasn't any of his business, but he couldn't help but feel the tiniest bit of jealousy.

Which was ridiculous! She was a grown woman, living on her own in the city. What boyfriends or lovers she had wasn't his business.

But still...

"You okay over there?" Chastity asked with a smile, already well into the barn. "You look like you're thinking deep thoughts."

"Nothing important," he said quickly, joining her in the barn. All of his family's horses were there in their stalls, some of them trotting to their doors in the hopes for a treat and some of them so relaxed in their pens that they clearly couldn't be bothered. He reminded himself to stay in the moment. After all, he was here with Chastity.

He was making up for lost time, so nothing else mattered.

"I don't suppose you brought any treats?" Chastity asked, looking sheepishly back at him.

Ben grinned. Some things never changed. "As a matter of fact," he said, walking over to the small fridge they had near the door, "I did prepare for this occasion."

Reaching in, he pulled out two bags that he had placed in

there that morning. One contained thick slices of apple, and the other, cubed pumpkin for some of the pickier horses. "There's enough in here for everyone," he said, handing her one of the bags. "I'll tell you who likes what."

She let out a happy sort of squeal and went right over to Gwen, his mother's oldest horse. She had been retired from riding long ago but still had plenty of life to her. Often when there was a colt who was a bit mean, they were put into her care, so she could teach them some manners. She hadn't gone wrong yet.

"Wait, I remember this one..." Chastity said, reaching out and stroking her head. "She's a bit grayer around the nose, but... is this your mom's?"

Ben nodded. "You got it. She's still kicking."

"Wow. What a matriarch."

"That's one way to put it." Ben said, laughing ever so lightly.

And down the line they went, feeding each one carefully, taking their time. For the friendlier horses, Chastity would rub their muzzles and scratch behind their ears, talking to them as if they were humans and could understand everything she was saying. The horses that were more ornery, she gave the appropriate distance.

He had always thought she was meant to be around animals. If he had ever met someone who was born for ranch life, it was her. All of the horses, even the less friendly ones, took to her, watching her with their large, honeyed eyes. He remembered being surprised at first—all those years ago—when she just waltzed in and made friends with every creature he introduced her to, but now he cherished it.

He realized that one of his ways of discouraging a money-hungry pursuer had been to bring the pursuer around the dirtiest parts of the ranch and the meanest animals they had.

Inevitably, they would always decide he was more trouble than his parents' fortune was worth. He'd never thought that Chastity had given him the idea, but seeing her laugh and coo at the horses reminded him how he had always been holding women up to a standard that he doubted any of them could ever reach.

After all, there was only one Chastity Parker. He had learned that lesson the hard way.

Eventually, however, they finished feeding the horses their treats, and when they stepped outside again, it was already dark. Before they could even reach the truck, Ben heard a sharp slap, and Chastity let out a light swear.

"I forgot how fast the mosquitos and horseflies descend. I don't suppose the rest of our date is indoors, is it?"

"It's not," Ben answered with a smirk. "But don't worry about that."

"Easy for you to say," she groused. "You're not the one being eaten alive."

He strode forward and opened the truck door for her. She huffed, but got in anyway, allowing him to close the door then go over to his side.

Once he was sure that she was belted in properly, he took off, bouncing over the vague roads that formed from him and his brothers crossing their lands. Only he and Benji had full-on trucks, the others usually preferred to use four-wheelers, but they all tended to walk the same paths.

Well, except for his younger brother. Ben couldn't remember the last time that he had been on the ranch to do any work, but hopefully he would shape up once his wild years passed.

At first, he had been tempted to take her to their old favorite date spot, but he then remembered that was where they broke up and quickly decided against it. Instead, he chose to take her to what was called Juniper's Grove. When they were younger, it had been overgrown with thistle and the like, but he and Benji had cleaned it out with the help of their father until it was a beautiful grove of weeping willows. Apparently, it was named after the daughter of the founding Miller, but he didn't know much about her beyond the fact that she was the independent type.

Not unlike a certain someone he knew...

He pulled up to the path that led to the grove and put the truck into park once again. Reaching over to Chastity, he noticed that she tensed. He felt himself smirk again as he opened the glove compartment and pulled out of a bottle of insect repellent.

"This should hold you over until we get to the spot," he said, handing it to her. "Spray outside the truck, please."

"Wow, you really did think of everything, didn't you?" she asked, seeming genuinely grateful.

"Perhaps. I guess we'll have to find out."

"Huh, when did you get all mysterious and dodgy?"

"I think you'll find that a lot of things have changed about me in my old age."

"Old age? You're thirty."

"I know. And my knees remind me every single morning."

She straight up snorted as they got out of the truck. On most people, perhaps that would be an unattractive sound, but on her, it seemed right. It was an honest sound, and that was what was so lacking in a lot of people he dealt with lately. Whether it was the man from the bank, or another woman looking to marry into the family, or distant buyers in other states, or competition who also claimed to have happy cattle but didn't treat their livestock with the same respect that the Millers did.

But he didn't have to worry about that with Chastity. If she felt something, she showed it. If she thought something, she spoke it. Even if she broke his heart, she was up-front with him.

He heard her spraying away outside of the truck and went out to the back, grabbing the cooler and backpack that he had prepped. He had been in shock when she agreed to the date. He was sure that she would shoot him down right there in front of her house. But since she *did* say yes, he'd spent the past three days preparing for it.

Once he had it all in hand, he went back around to her side and saw her finishing up her insect-repellant shower. He remembered how once she had gone camping with his family, sleeping in her own tent next to his parents with another girl from school, whom she was trying to make friends with, and she had awoken with bright red bumps all up and down both her legs and arms. They really did seem to like her blood.

"Ready?" he asked, looking her over.

Even in the starlight, she was radiant. He remembered the first time that he saw her. He was a freshman, and she suddenly appeared in his grade one day. She was wearing simple jeans and an oversized T-shirt, with her dark hair in a bun, but his eyes had been glued to her. She had these broad, lovely cheekbones that always seemed to catch the light, and her eyes were a different shape than everyone else's. Her skin wasn't as tanned as some of the girls who hit the town's only tanning salon, but it was a different color, one that spoke of horseback rides in the sunset and summers spent in the fields.

He remembered asking around to see if anyone knew her, and by the end of the day, he knew that she was a younger student that had tested two years higher during eighth grade and had been shuttled up to freshman year. Unfortunately, that meant that she was either twelve or thirteen, depending on her birthday and since Ben was the ripe old age of fifteen, Ben knew that she was too young for him.

So, he settled on being friends. Not that friendship with Chastity was settling in any way, as he soon found out. With her, often everything was an adventure, and she had this stark ambition for life that he admired. Her family was poor, and her parents' views were traditional, so he knew practically from day one that she was out to make better than most people would expect of her. Because people expected so little of her.

It was strange, really. Just because of her parents' money issues and the fact that she was one half Native American, and it showed, people thought they could make certain comments to her. They were never outright enough to get them fired, reprimanded, or scolded, but they were enough for Chastity to know that they thought of her as different. Whether it was a remark about being "off the rez"—or returning to it—or "avoiding the vices of her people," or asking if she was going to try to get a job at the casino a city over. Ben remembered seeing these remarks steel her resolve instead of crumbling it, but he couldn't help but want to shoulder that pain for her.

Unfortunately, often all his teenaged self could do was listen. So, he did. The two of them became thick as thieves, and it was in sophomore year, after her fourteenth birthday and while he was still fifteen, that he asked her out. The age difference seemed less important when they were only a year apart —even if his own birthday was just two months later.

That was how it all began. Four years of knowing each other and three years of dating, before it all slipped through his fingers. And now, looking at her bathed in starlight, he recognized that he still felt much of the same way as he did back then

—enraptured by the beauty and force of nature that encompassed everything she was.

There was never going to be another Chastity, was there?

"Ready!" she answered with a bright smile. That smile. Man, how he had always loved that smile. It seemed like nothing could be wrong with the world when she was grinning at him like that.

Ben would have liked to offer his arm, but he was quite loaded up at the moment, so instead he gave her a nod and walked past her, through the weeping willow grove where it quickly grew dark. Thankfully, Chastity lit up the bowed trees with her cellphone, and they made it to their destination.

Looking to Chastity, he hoped that she could feel the natural serenity of this place. And maybe, just maybe, how he still felt for her.

But that was probably too much to hope for.

16

Chastity

*C*hastity looked around at the beautiful grove he had taken her to. She had somehow never been to this part of the ranch before, but it was utterly breathtaking. Weeping willows bowed on either side of a comfortable, circular clearing, just big enough for a few people. The leaves hung from the tree's slender whips, glittering silver in the moonlight.

There were two gaps in the thick circle of green, one being the entrance with a beautiful, vine covered trellis, and the other overlooking one of the many large ponds that the ducks and geese loved to nest around.

"Wow," Chastity said the word in awe, as he led her to a fire circle. "How do I not remember this?"

"It didn't look quite this good in our days back on the ranch."

Chastity's breath caught for a moment, and he looked back at her curiously.

"What is it? Did you see something?" he asked.

"No. It's just... it's silly."

He set down the cooler and the backpack, unzipping the latter to pull out a soft, thick blanket that she was pretty sure his mom had probably knitted herself. That woman was amazing with a needle. "What? Come on, now I want to know what you were thinking."

"I dunno. It was hearing you call it our days. It was..." Romantic? Moving? Nostalgic? "...weird."

"Hah. Sorry about that. I guess I could refer to it as the time in which you and I used to be involved. More of a mouthful though."

"It's fine," Chastity said, settling on the very edge of the blanket and starting to build up the center part of the fire. She loved building bonfires and took pride in being skilled at it. Of course, Ben was the one who taught her, so it was mostly his doing, but still. That didn't stop her from enjoying the meticulous process nonetheless. "Don't worry about it."

"No, that's your job."

She looked up sharply. "What do you mean by that?"

The corner of his mouth went up in that lightly teasing way of his. "Between the two of us, who do you guess overthinks things more?"

She laughed at that, feeling herself relax. Even after all this time, they still had their same sort of bantering rhythm. "Oh, you may have a point."

Although Ben had never been a huge talker, he always had been quick-witted around her. It was one of the things that drew her to him. He knew how to make her laugh.

He also knew how to end a conversation with infuriating skill.

"Glad you think so."

He settled down further back from her, and she heard him pulling several things out of the cooler. She was sure that they were probably delicious and way more expensive than anything that she could afford. Once the structure of the fire was fully ready, she leaned back, her hand out.

"You got a lighter?" she asked.

"You know, typically the gentleman does all the preparation."

"Yeah, and typically the lady doesn't have a proclivity for pyrotechnics."

"That always was a bit concerning. I don't need to look up arson reports in the Big Apple, do I?"

Chastity laughed, tilting her head back. "You've found me out."

"And here in this good, Christian country? What a scandal."

"It wouldn't be our first. Remember when we went to the Snow Ball together?"

Ben chuckled lightly as he passed her a long lighter. "Oh, I remember. There were a lot of accusations of robbing the cradle and if we had your parents' permission."

"You would have thought I was twelve, not fourteen."

Ben shrugged, but Chastity didn't miss the smile around his lips. "Well, I had just turned sixteen a couple of months before, so I understand the concern they had that I might have been taking advantage of you."

Chastity couldn't help but laugh again. "Hah, can you imagine me letting anyone take advantage of me?"

Ben shook his head. "Judging by your right hook? No, I can't."

"And that's after calming down over the past decade. I used to be a real spitfire."

"Used to be?"

She tossed the lighter at his head, the fire beginning to flicker to life in the kindling. "I'm a right proper lady now, I'll have you know. I'm almost thirty."

"And I *am* thirty," his eyes narrowed. "Which means your birthday is coming up soon."

"Yup, and for a slight bit of time, you will only be a year older than me."

"And then that will quickly end as I turn thirty-one."

"Yes, that is how math works...last I checked."

"Cheeky."

Finally, she turned around, a pithy response ready, but her words stalled as she saw the spread he had prepared for them, all of the containers already open.

There was a bottle of champagne and four bottles of what looked like half-frozen water. He remembered how much she liked water with her meals. That was nice.

In the center was what looked like a roast pheasant, stuffed with a decadent rice that smelled both sweet and savory. There was a side of mashed potatoes, and she didn't need a time machine to remember how delicious his mother's dish was. There was also corn on the cob, some greens, and even a small platter of ribs. It all looked mouthwatering, and she had to swallow quickly to stop herself from drooling.

"You like?" Ben asked, looking at her over the spread as he pulled out two of those special candles that she knew repelled bugs. He lit them and gently placed them on either side of the blanket, far enough away from the edge not to be a fire hazard, but close enough to repel the insects—and give it a romantic feel.

"I like," Chastity answered honestly. Her heart was thumping in her chest and her palms were sweaty. It felt like there was a heavy but welcome presence in the air, one that made every moment, every interaction that much more special.

She knew she should probably resist the emotions swirling through her and tell herself that she was caught up in the magic of the ranch and its open plains, but for once she let herself enjoy the moment.

That couldn't be so wrong, could it?

"Are you ready to dig in?" Ben asked, looking to her hopefully.

"What, and no prayer?"

He shrugged again, his muscled shoulders rolling under his shirt. "You're here. God's already answered all of them."

Oh.

Oh wow.

Chastity stared at him, eyes wide, before reacting with a snicker. "Did you work on that line all day or—"

"What would you like on your plate?" he interrupted, grabbing one of the plates he had brought from the backpack.

But Chastity wasn't willing to let him off that easily. "You always were a bit of a hopeless romantic, weren't you?"

"I know many people who would disagree emphatically with you on that."

"Uh-huh, and how many of those people were after your money and you sniffed them out first?"

"Fair."

"I'll take a little of everything, by the way, and a huge helping of your mom's potatoes."

"How do you know I didn't make these?"

"Because you're not insane and only a madman would miss out on a chance to eat Ma Miller's mashed 'taters."

"You may have a point there. But I'll have you know that Benji is learning how to make them, so we all won't be screwed once she's gone."

"Oh? Maybe I should be on a date with him then," she joked.

Ben stopped scooping for a moment, seeming to consider her words. "I don't think I would like that."

"Would you be jealous?"

"...yes. I believe so."

That was certainly something. The Miller brothers were known as an unshakable crew that shared everything and rarely ever fought. Sure, they got irritated with each other and had little squabbles, but—all in all—they were a loving unit. For Ben to admit that he might harbor negative feelings toward his brother over her... well, it was something.

"Well, don't worry. I don't think I'll be dating anyone anytime soon."

"You're on a date now."

"You know what I mean." She took the plate as he handed it to her, along with the glass of champagne, and the water bottle too.

"What if I don't?"

She rolled her eyes, but the pleasant feeling didn't stop. There was something about the way Ben looked at her that made her feel so cherished. Like she was one of a kind that he would never see again. While Chastity didn't normally like to think of herself as vain or a romantic, she couldn't deny the way he made her feel.

It had been ten years, but as she stared into his eyes, she wondered if she had ever fallen out of love with the eldest Miller son. From the muscles and veins in his forearms, to the thick column of his neck, to his tanned face with all of the classically strong Miller traits. He was handsome. He was kind. And he treated her better than anyone else did.

Why did it have to end?

Because he had his life here, and she couldn't have hers. There was so much more out there, and she wanted to try it all. She couldn't be a doting housewife with no skills other than popping out babies. Not that there was anything wrong with that, but it was always what her parents told her she was meant for, so she resented the idea entirely.

But that wasn't Ben's fault. Maybe they could work something out... No! No, she wasn't going down that path. That would lead to heartbreak and all sorts of emotions she didn't want. After all, she was going to go back to the city and live her life, but with much more energy and hope than she had before. She couldn't break his heart again by letting him think they would amount to anything, and then just disappear with the wind.

That would be too cruel.

"You all right? You have that look on your face."

"What look?"

"The one you get when you're overthinking something."

"I didn't know that was a look."

His nose crinkled as his smile grew broader, and her heart skipped a beat. Wow, how did he look so happy? A bright, shining star in a world filled with a whole lot of uncertainty and darkness. "It's definitely a look. I can see it in your eyes."

Well, she might as well tell him. "Well, I was thinking of how nice this was, and I'm going to miss it when I go back to the city. Because I *am* going to go back."

He nodded, and she could see the muscles of his face tensing and relaxing, as if he was physically working out his words. "Why do you have to go back?"

"Because I have a life there. A destiny."

"A destiny?"

She nodded. "You remember. Ever since I was little, people thought I would either end up as a casino worker or an unwed mother. People out here like to think that they're progressive, but some of them still call us 'Injuns' or 'Redskins.'" Chastity rolled her eyes, then continued.

"And as for the ones that weren't racist, they saw us together and assumed I was all about becoming a gold-digging mother to the next generation of Miller spawn."

"Spawn. That's not a great name for kids."

"But it's accurate."

Ben sighed, and Chastity was sure that he was going to try to convince her how wrong she was. "I understand."

"You do?" she asked.

"Of course, I do." His green eyes stared at her, seeming to take in every feature of her face and soul. "Chastity, you're the most determined woman I've ever met. If someone tells you no, you take that as a challenge to try harder. I should have known better than to think you could ever settle for a future with just me."

Ow.

Without thinking, she found herself reaching out to him, her hands settling over his. "Please don't think about it that way. A life with you isn't some consolation prize. You're a wonderful, loving man. Building a life with you would be more than most people could ask for."

"But not more than you could ask for?"

She shook her head slowly, feeling her heart sink within her as she spoke the truth. It quelled the romantic, fairy-tale feelings within her, but it needed to be said. "No, it's not enough."

Silence stretched out between them for several moments,

the only point of contact between them being the sun that was contained between their hands. Chastity wished she could comfort him in this moment, and yet she was the one causing his pain.

"I think I've found a new prayer," he said eventually, his voice just a low rumble that sent chills up her spine.

"Have you?"

He nodded. "I think I'll pray that maybe, someday, it will be enough."

She didn't know if that was something that she should encourage, or if she should shut all of this down right now, but her heart ached for him.

How was he single after all these years? He was such a handsome, considerate, lovely man. There had to be dozens of women in town pining after him, wishing they could somehow catch his eye. And yet he seemed to be stuck on her, a lost woman with wanderlust carved into her very bones and a rampant desire for *more.*

Always more.

She wasn't thinking clearly. Fueled by emotion and the drive to make him stop looking so gosh-darned hurt, she found herself up on her knees, her plate flipped to its side. She drew in a sharp breath, and then her lips were on his, pressing into his soft skin.

Could he feel it? How much she wanted their fairy tale to be true? How she wished she could settle in his arms and forget her drive and ambitions?

He seemed to, because his arms wrapped around her middle and crushed her to him. And for a moment, there was nothing else. Just them, and their lips moving against each other, clinging to the humanity that connected them so intensely.

Kissing him was better than anything else she could ever imagine. It made her blood rush and her skin flush and her head spin in the best way possible. She loved the feeling, everything about it.

Suddenly, he was pulling her even farther, leaning back until he was on the ground, then rolling so that she was under him. His hands moved from behind her, instead caressing her sides and legs. He took care to stay away from any zone that was too dangerous, but it was clear that he wanted to feel all of her.

And she wanted to be felt. After so many years of protecting herself in the city, of maintaining a proper distance and never trusting, she wanted to be close to the one man who always seemed to understand her.

They continued to kiss, attraction, affection, and love drenching them in its honey-sweet wine. For several moments, she was lost, forgetting about the city and the grand destiny she had in her mind—and everything else.

Until her phone rang with a shrill tone.

That jolted her from the moment, and she pushed Ben off, reaching down into her pocket to yank her phone out. She clicked the answer button before it was even to her ear, her heart racing in an entirely different way.

"Hello?" she asked, although she knew that ringtone only belonged to her mother.

Except it wasn't her mother. It was an entirely different woman altogether.

"Hello? Ms. Parker?"

"Yes, this is she."

"Hello, this is your mother's night nurse." Ah, right. That made sense.

Chastity cut right down to the heart of the matter. "Is my mother all right?"

"Physically, yes, but she apparently had a dream that her husband was just off at the store, and when she woke up, she realized the truth. She's very much beside herself now, and I think she would do well with you here."

"Absolutely. I'll be there as fast as I can."

She looked up at Ben with guilt in her eyes, but he was already on his feet, looking quite worried. "Your mother?" he asked.

She nodded, the mood shattered as he pulled her upright. She would have plenty of time to scold herself later, but for now all she was worried about was her mom.

"Let's get you home then."

They gathered everything up and walked quickly to the car, saying nothing. And when they sped onto the roads, going far faster than they probably should, they were still quiet.

Ben got her to her house in record time, and she erupted from his car before he could even open the door. He shouted out to her to call him if she needed a single thing, and she nodded before disappearing through her door, grateful that he understood that tonight wasn't something that he could aid with.

But as the door closed and she rushed upstairs to her mom, Chastity couldn't help but wonder if they had crossed a line they shouldn't have.

Oh well. That could wait until later. Right now, there were more pressing things at hand.

17

Chastity

*T*he dream that interrupted Chastity's date with Ben was a catalyst for Chastity's mom, because suddenly her mental state began to tank. Instead of being mostly lucid with moments of confusion, she became generally dazed with only a few instances of clarity a day. It was exhausting, and after a few days of it, Chastity called the doctor.

She had some good news. Apparently, it wasn't Alzheimer's or brain cancer, which was really the only positive parts of the message. Unfortunately, it was dementia and they needed to do more tests to figure out what kind exactly—which meant more co-pays and more office visits, but their bank account was pretty much bled dry. Chastity only had one more month on her phone before they shut it off, and she still hadn't found a job.

More than once she found herself thinking of how unfair it

all was, but that was unproductive and a waste of energy, so she tried to turn off the negative thoughts.

That proved difficult, however, as troubles kept mounting and mounting. She felt like she was drowning and there wasn't a life raft in sight.

"Chastity, dear. I'd like to go to church."

Chastity looked up from the classifieds, where she was highlighting all of the odd jobs and hiring postings that sounded like they were something she could do. She was desperate, and yet she couldn't bring herself to ask Ben for money. That seemed so wrong.

"Can we do that next week, Mom? I have a lot to do and catch up on."

The rest of her things had arrived from the service she had used to deliver them from storage, and she was listing them online, hoping maybe they could net her some money to get them by. She didn't have a ton, but she had collected enough stuff over the past decade to maybe get them by a month or two if she sold most of it.

"Oh, a week from now is a long way away. Could we try to go to the Wednesday night Bible study? I really do feel the need to be sharpened."

"Sharpened?" Chastity repeated, looking back to the classifieds she had spread over the table.

"Yes. As it says in the Bible, real life can dull us up, and I feel awfully dull. We're all supposed to sharpen ourselves in the Lord."

"Huh. Sounds weird, but I believe you."

"It's not weird, Chastity. It's the Lord's word."

"I'm sure it is. But I have to make sure that we have enough to keep up with the bills, so we'll see where we are on Wednesday, okay?"

"Okay," she said with a nod. "I'll pray that it all falls into place."

"In this case, I don't think that anything will fall into place. It's all about hard work and using the resources that he's given us."

"Ah, true, true. You know what they say about idle hands."

She tottered off to make tea, and Chastity delved into her work. Even if everything went perfectly, she would be stuck paying the very minimum payment on all their bills, and they would have a meager thirty dollars left over for groceries.

And that wasn't for the week. Chastity had done all right on less than that for a week before. No, it was thirty dollars for the month, and then they would have nothing for copays.

UGH. She needed a job.

This small-town search wasn't working for her. Like that boy from high school said, most of the places knew who she was and that she had left town for a decade without looking back. They thought this meant that she wasn't trustworthy and that she would skip out again, or that a local deserved the spot more than her.

If she was going to make money, she needed to look online.

"Hey, Mom, are you going to be all right if I dip out for an hour and a half?"

"Of course, dear, I'm not a child. That will give me time to make some tea and sandwiches for a late lunch. I trust you're not hungry yet and can wait until you're back?"

"Yes, that sounds lovely. You know to call me if you need anything."

"That I do. But I'll be fine, really."

Chastity ground her teeth nervously. Leaving her mother alone in her deteriorating state was a gamble. She seemed fine now, but what if she left the oven on? Or set something on top of the stove that she shouldn't? Or forgot that she was cooking at all?

But they needed money, and she couldn't rely on the charity of others to get them through, especially others who just so happened to be her ex from high school that she had just kissed in a torrid burst of passion a couple days previous.

She glanced to her phone as she packed up. Maybe she should text him? But what would she say? Her heart did its own special little throb when she remembered that moment, his weight pressed to her as their lips locked and their bodies spoke an entirely new language together.

It was like how it used to be between them, and yet there was something else to it. A sort of intensity they didn't have as teenagers. If they had, she didn't think that they ever would have gone to their classes and would have spent their days in sin.

These feelings were dangerous—and complicated. Perhaps it would be better if she didn't ever message him again.

Yeah right, as if she would be able to resist doing that.

That was something she could worry about after she got their financial situation more in order. Finishing packing up her laptop, a water bottle, her phone, and her charger, she headed out the door.

Just like everything else in town, the library was within a ten-minute walk. She checked in with the librarian to see if there had been any progress on her application, and after a vague, noncommittal answer that meant they really weren't interested, she headed over to one of the sitting areas.

She didn't have a moment to waste, so she searched for different ways to make money online. Of course, pornography came up first, but she skipped past those.

Hmm, surveys online? That seemed like something. It wouldn't be enough to survive off of, but maybe it could help bolster their grocery bill for the month. But who knew, considering she would only have an hour every other day or so. If only her parents had Wi-Fi...

Maybe she could do some on her phone? That would certainly help. Might even help her go to sleep, considering most nights she was afraid she'd awaken to her mother crying again.

Chastity had been through some rough things, but nothing quite compared to watching her mother sob over her father, remembering that he was dead all over again. It had been a heartbreaking, soul-destroying sound, and Chastity could go her entire life without ever having to hear *that* again.

It was easy enough to get started, and she found herself quickly going through surveys, her high reading speed working to her advantage. They were only five cents, ten cents, occasionally twenty cents a pop, but at least it was something. She would continue looking tomorrow for more profitable work, but at least this was giving her a baseline.

All too soon, an hour had passed, and it was time to pack up and head right back home. She'd only earned five dollars, but at least it was a start. If she could get it on her phone, she could probably whack out another dollar or two throughout the day and before she went to sleep.

Hope bubbled up a little, even though seven dollars a day wasn't nearly enough to cover their expenses. But as long as they had food, it couldn't be too bad, could it?

Those thoughts plagued her, but she shucked them out of her mind before she walked through the front door at home. She didn't want her mother to pick up on her mood and have an episode. In the weeks that she had been home, she had noticed her mother's incidents did indeed increase toward the evening. Whether it was because she was tired and stressed from the day, or because something to do with the sun or darkness, Chastity didn't know. All she knew was that a month had come and gone, and she was nowhere near being in a position where she could go back to the city.

"Chastity dear, is that you?"

"Of course, who else would it be?" she answered, kicking off her shoes as she went inside.

"I don't know. Hopefully not that horrible bank man."

Chastity chuckled slightly at that. "I don't think he'll be bothering us. Ben made sure of that."

"Ben? Is that a friend you made in town?"

Chastity was no longer surprised by instances like these. "Yeah, he is."

"Ah, well I'm so glad you're trying to fit in again. I've made some grilled cheese and potato soup, if you're hungry."

"That I am! Thank you, Mom."

"Don't worry about it. It's nice to take care of my little girl again. I'm starvin'."

"I bet you are. You get up at seven a.m. Lunch at three is a bit late for you."

"But it was worth the wait to sit and have lunch with my daughter. Now you sit down—I have your plate all ready."

Chastity did so, and soon her mother joined her with steaming food for both of them. They sat across from each other, and conversation flowed easily. This was what she loved about being with her mother. The memories that she would cherish for years to come. This was why she did this. Why she stayed.

She knew she was making the right decision, even if it was a hard one.

18

Chastity

*C*hastity awoke in a cold sweat, her nightmares trying to keep a hold on her as she rocketed into the real world. It seemed that her mother's penchant for unpleasant dreams was leaking into her own mind, because her stomach was still flipping from whatever nastiness had been going on in her head—even if it was already fleeing from her memories.

She didn't have time to linger on that, however, because she had a lot to do. It was time for more of the tests for her mom, and like the knight in shining armor he was, Ben was going to be arriving on his silver steed to take them to the city.

So much for not calling him.

She hoped that he didn't feel like she was using him; he was just one of the only people she knew in town who had the means to take them to the city and wouldn't suffer from giving up so many hours of his day sitting around.

Ugh. She hated being reliant on people, but she was incredibly grateful. Her mother would be a lot worse off if it weren't for the Miller family. She definitely owed them a debt. Not that they would ever think of it that way. They were just that kind of people.

She went through her morning, getting herself and her mother ready. Mom was being especially curmudgeonly that morning, refusing to do a lot of simple tasks, but at least Chastity managed to get her dressed by the time she got Ben's text. Leading her mother downstairs, she helped her to the door.

Immediately upon seeing Ben, her mother's face brightened.

"Oh, it's you again," she said with one of the brightest smiles that she had worn in days.

"Yes, it's me, your humble chauffeur." Ben gave a dramatic sort of bow that reminded her of some of the plays they did together. "Are you ready to ride to the city?"

"I do think I am," she answered, letting go of Chastity and taking his strong arm. "It's not every day that a woman gets such a handsome escort."

"Handsome? Well, I don't know about that." He laughed and the sound put Chastity at ease. She really was lucky to have him in her life, even if the last time they had parted had been abrupt.

Chastity closed the door and headed toward the back seat when Ben turned to her. "Hey, why don't you stay here? I know you have a lot of work to do, and you could use a morning to yourself."

She stared at him with wide eyes. "Oh, no but thank you. Mother—"

"Don't use me as an excuse," Mrs. Parker said, leaning out of the door as Ben helped her up. "I'm fine with this young man taking me. You're cranky enough lately that you could use a good nap."

"What? I'm not cranky."

"Ya see that right there?" her mother continued, laying her southern drawl on thicker than usual. "You're tired."

But it was Ben's kind hand on her shoulder that gave her pause. "Trust me, Chastity. I can take care of this. You go do whatever you need to do. Take time for yourself. *Please*?"

How could she say no to that? Besides, four whole hours of doing surveys and searching for other ways to make a couple bucks would be fantastic. That's about as much as she'd done in the entire last week.

"...I guess I could."

"That's my girl," her mother said with a mischievous smile. If Chastity didn't know better, she would think that the woman was angling to flirt with Ben. Hopefully, she didn't mistake him for Charles and was just having fun in a potentially stressful situation.

"I'll see you later. I promise I will call if anything happens."

"Are you sure we should do this? You're not her power of attorney."

"I'll have them call you if they need to. But I think your mother's in a good state today."

"What are the two of you talking about over there?" her mother called, leaning out of the door again.

"Just saying goodbye," Ben said before turning to me and winking. "You be good now, Chastity."

"When am I not?" Chastity shot back.

"Do you really want me to answer that?"

"Fair point."

They got into the car and drove off, leaving Chastity watching after them. She stood there for a few moments, worried if she had made the wrong decision, before kicking herself out of that. She had been given the gift of several hours to get some work done, and by golly if she wasn't going to use that to the fullest.

It was a mad dash to get all of her stuff then power walk over to the library. She was tempted to run, but she knew that she would get sweaty and overheated then lose precious minutes lowering her heart rate. Even though she loved running to relax herself late at night, she didn't like doing any sort of intense physical activity when she was expected to be in public shortly after.

She arrived in good time and sat at her now usual spot. It seemed people rarely used this part of the small library, so it gave her plenty of privacy to concentrate. She booted up her computer and started in on the highest paying surveys, whacking them out as quickly and efficiently as she could.

But after an hour's work, she figured it was time for a break from filling out surveys to look into other money-making schemes. During her search, she found a website that did lists for clickbait articles and another site for audio transcription. She loved the idea and signed up for the former before applying to the second. Apparently, that one would take about two weeks for them to get back to her.

It took a bit of internet surfing to figure out the list-making, but she managed, and about twenty minutes later, she was starting on her first list. She figured she would stick with what she knew and picked ten places to go in NYC on a budget.

It was more involved than doing a survey, that was for sure, but it paid ten dollars as a base line and then five dollars more per milestone that the article reached in number of hits. If she was lucky, maybe she'd end up with about thirty dollars on one list alone. The higher tiers went up to several hundreds of dollars, but she doubted that she would get that high on her first crack.

Once she was completely sure her list was ready to submit, she did so, then went right back to her surveys.

It wasn't very exciting stuff, but at least she was being productive, and that helped fuel her. She kept on going until her eyes crossed, and then she hunted around for another article idea. Top Ten Reasons to Visit Montana? Maybe. That was certainly something she was knowledgeable about. But the best part was for this whole article thing, she didn't have to be online to work on it, only to submit. So, she could spend time at home writing things up, then come to the library to upload them and sneak in a few surveys.

Things really were coming together, and she recognized that they wouldn't have if it weren't for Ben agreeing to take her mother to the city alone. She didn't know how she would ever repay him, but she—

As if he was psychic, her phone buzzed. No one really messaged her besides Ben, her mother, and the doctor, so she picked it up instantly. Ben had texted that they were almost home and were stopping for gas, as well as asking if she wanted a soda.

Naturally, Chastity replied that she did. She generally didn't drink soft drinks, as they were an extra cost and made her repeatedly go to the bathroom, but she knew several of the gas stations around the town carried old-fashioned cream soda in glass bottles. She'd have to be insane to pass that up.

Once she was sure that her list had been submitted and her texted response to Ben had gone through, she packed up her things and headed home. She ended up taking a couple of extra minutes, as the librarian stopped her to talk about the job she had applied for. It turned out one of their book shelvers was pregnant and having a hard time of it, so there could possibly be an opening in a couple of weeks. They would let her know.

It took her about twenty minutes to get home, and when she got there, she saw Ben's truck already pulled up in front.

Despite herself, this time she really did run, bolting up the steps and almost throwing open the door. There, she was surprised not to see the strapping man, but instead, she saw Mrs. Miller sitting at the table with her mother, sipping at willow bark tea and reading the Bible together.

"Oh, Chastity. Hello. It's good to see you," Mrs. Miller said, and Chastity could immediately place her as the kind voice on the phone who had gotten this ball rolling all those weeks ago. What would have happened if she hadn't made that call? Probably nothing good.

"It's good to see you as well, Mrs. Miller. You look as lovely as ever."

"Oh, you flatterer," she said, covering her face slightly and waving the compliment away. "But thank you nonetheless."

"Why don't I get compliments like that?" her mom asked teasingly, pretending to pout.

"Well Mom, that's because I'm a reflection of you, and what better compliment could you be paid?"

"Oh, *cheeky* now. That you get from your father." Although she was smiling, the expression faltered slightly. Thankfully, Mrs. Miller noticed and reached over to pat her mother's hand comfortingly. The two older women interlaced their fingers, and Chastity felt tears prickle in her eyes as they looked at each other in a knowing way.

After all these weeks, she had never thought that maybe her

mother would benefit from hanging out with someone her age. That was definitely lack of foresight on her side of things, and she resolved to set up play dates for her mother. It seemed so obvious now, but oh well, she couldn't exactly go into the past and fix it.

Chastity sidled up to Ben, feeling far more relaxed about her future than she had in weeks. "Thank you," she said in a hushed voice, not wanting to interrupt their mothers as they settled back into the Bible.

"I didn't do anything. This was all my mother's idea." Ben handed her a bottle of cream soda.

"Thank you. Was it?" Chastity asked. "*All* of it?" She took a sip from the bottle and moaned as the delicious cream soda touched her taste buds.

He shrugged and chuckled at her reaction to the soda. "I may have asked her if she wanted to come to the doctor's office with us, but the rest was all her doing."

"That sounds like it. This is a Miller family affair if I ever saw one."

"You make us sound like roving philanthropists."

"Well, your whole fortune is built on top of treating your animals better than almost all other farms this side of the St. Louis Arch." Chastity took another sip from the bottle and licked her lips.

"Not our whole fortune, but I get your meaning."

"Enough of your fortune. Besides, when did you get so particular about the semantics?"

"Who do you think I learned it from?" He gave her an accusatory look, and she just batted her eyelashes at him.

"I have no idea what you mean."

"Of course, you don't."

They sank into a comfortable sort of silence as their

mothers continued to read to each other, and soon a whole hour had passed. At that time, Mrs. Miller looked up from the Bible and affixed them with a smile. "I think it's about time that I should head home. The chickens need tending to and goodness knows your father is probably out with the firewood much longer than he should be again."

"Oh Annie, I hope I didn't keep you too long," Chastity's mom said, concern written across her face.

"Not at all. You kept me the perfect amount of time. We should do this again, perhaps next week if we have the chance?"

"Oh yes, I would like that very much."

"Perfect." Mrs. Miller looked to Ben. "And are you ready to go?"

He looked to Chastity and seemed to be unsure whether to hug or kiss her or shake her hand. She smirked a bit before solving it for him, standing on her tip toes to press a chaste kiss to his cheek.

"Thank you, for everything."

He smiled, his face flushing slightly, and he winked one of those sparkling green eyes at her, flecks of gold within catching the fluorescent light overhead.

"It was nothing. Really."

"It was to me," Chastity said.

She walked with him to the door, almost wanting to slip her hand into his large, calloused one, but that didn't seem right at the moment. She watched them go, not closing the door until they had driven down the road and out of sight.

"That was lovely," her mother said, humming happily to herself.

"I'm happy you had a nice visit. Are you thirsty? My soda was so sweet I need some water."

"I could use a cup of water too."

Chastity crossed to the fridge, grabbing two of their chilled glasses from the freezer. It was a habit that her mother had gotten her into when she was younger, and now she lived for a glass of refrigerated water in a chilled cup.

But when she opened the fridge door, she could only stand there in shock.

"Oh."

She didn't have any other words for what she saw. In front of her, their entire fridge was filled to the absolute brim with a variety of food.

Most of it was cooked and neatly tucked into expensive Tupperware. She could make out ribs, roasted chicken, tenderloins, sausage, bacon, and each of them had labels of the date they were made and how long they could be kept. Of course, right in the center of it was a giant container of mashed potatoes. It seemed after all these years, Mrs. Miller still knew her well.

But that was just the cooked food. There were also plenty of raw vegetables and fruits, as well as breadstuffs and deli meat.

"What is this?"

"What is what?"

"We have an entire fridge full of food. Surely, you noticed."

"Oh, that. Annie wanted to give us a bit of a gift. She is such a lovely soul, isn't she?"

Chastity's heart throbbed in her chest. After so long being on her own, it was entirely strange to realize that she still had people watching out for her.

Even after their breakup, even after their suddenly interrupted kiss, even after her radio silence, Ben was still trying to help in what little ways he could.

She really didn't deserve him.

Life was going to suck when she went back to the city.

But for now, with her mother's condition making her stay longer and for an unknown length of time, would it really be so bad to enjoy the few good things that were happening to her?

She hoped not.

19

Ben

*B*en smiled to himself as he pulled up to the main house, helping his mother out of his truck. The morning really had gone splendidly, and it was hard to believe that it wasn't even three in the afternoon yet.

He guessed that Chastity was right; he still was a bit of a romantic. When she had called, needing a ride for her mother to go into the city, he had started to put together a plan to make her smile. Even through the phone, it was easy to hear how stressed she was and how bad she felt asking him for another favor when she hadn't spoken to him since their rather heated kiss on their date.

But he understood that too. Judging by the visit from that awful bank man, it was clear that there were a lot of pieces she was picking up for her mother after her father's death. And although Ben would like to help her with those too, he understood that she didn't want to involve him.

He was, after all, still her ex.

Even if kissing her *had* felt like the world turning upside down and the sun coming out after a decade of darkness.

To his surprise, his phone rang on the way to his bachelor add-on to the main house. It was far too early for any of his brothers to be calling unless it was an emergency, so he quickly answered without even looking at the number.

"Hello?"

"Hey, Ben."

Chastity. One of the last people he expected, but she was a welcome surprise. She sounded much less stressed than the last time she had called, and he couldn't help but feel a bit cocky that his plan had worked.

"Hey, Chastity. Did you need something?"

"No. I'm calling to thank you, again. I saw what you did in the kitchen."

"Huh? I assure you I have absolutely no idea of what you mean."

"Yeah, I'm sure you don't. Then I suppose it's going to be very strange when I ask you over for dinner sometime later in the week? Maybe I can cook you something nice with all the food you've given us—as a thank you."

Ben smiled to himself. "I don't know what food you're talking about, but I would be lying if I said that didn't sound like a good time."

"Good. I'll see you Thursday then, at seven? That's not too late for you, is it?"

"No, it's not."

"All right then. You have a good night now."

"I will, you too."

She paused like she was going to hang up, but then her voice came back uncertainly. "Uh, Ben?"

"Yes?"

"Sweet dreams."

It was a throwback to what she used to tell him before they bid each other goodnight, and he found himself smiling into his phone. "Sweet dreams to you too."

He hung up, staring at his phone, wondering if he was as in love now as he was back then.

This was probably a bad idea, but there was no stopping it now.

BEN'S HEART was pounding almost painfully behind his ribs as he approached Chastity's door. For some reason, he was even more nervous now than he had been on their first date together after a decade. Maybe it was because it was on her terms, and he couldn't meticulously orchestrate everything like he had on their last date.

Or maybe it was because he was realizing how intense his feelings were rapidly becoming. He really needed to put the brakes on—after all, she had told him that she fully intended on leaving their town—but he found himself enjoying the freefall. It was certainly going to be a painful lesson to learn the second time around, and yet there he was, knocking on her door with a bottle of expensive wine in his free hand.

Chastity answered the door, and it took quite a bit of resolve for his jaw not to entirely drop. She was wearing one of those form-fitting dresses that had become popular of late, bodycons, or something, and it was a beautiful turquoise against her golden skin. Her makeup was fancier than it had been on their first date, and her hair was meticulously curled.

"You look gorgeous," he said, knowing he should smile or make some sort of expression with his face but completely unable to from the shock of how unimaginably breathtaking she was.

"Thank you. You look pretty nice yourself."

He looked down at his pair of non-torn jeans, a clean button-up, and brown boots. Hardly. He should have dressed himself even more for her, but he wasn't sure if there really was a level between casual and a suit for men. He had never really been into fashion or designer stuff like his younger brother was. What was the term? Metro-something?

"Come in," Chastity said, stepping to the side. He saw that the table had already been set and in the center of it was a hearty roast, and he was pretty sure he could smell something sweet lingering in the air.

"Is that huckleberry pie?" he asked, striding over to the table and setting the bottle of wine down.

"Indeed, it is. I remember that was your favorite, wasn't it?"

He smiled back at her, pleased as punch. He did indeed love huckleberry pie, but didn't indulge in it often because his brother, Bart had been quite allergic to the berries and it wasn't worth the risk.

"Yes, and it still is." He almost sat down before remembering his manners, and so he circled around the table to pull her chair out for her. Chastity just laughed, her cheeks blushing slightly.

"I'm not quite ready for that yet. I was heating up some of your mother's mashed potatoes, and I'm finishing up the corn."

"Oh, well, I can keep you company in the kitchen while you finish."

Her smile was soft and welcoming as she looked up at him. He wanted to bend down and kiss her right then and there, but he resisted. He had a feeling that if their lips touched the dinner would be entirely forgotten, and he didn't want all her considerate effort to go to waste.

Besides, if he remembered correctly, Chastity was almost as good of a cook as her mother, having taken over for her family during the summers when school was out. She said that it helped her relax, but he was pretty sure that her type-A personality wanted to see the reward of a smile on people's face after they ate what she had made.

"That sounds nice."

They headed over to the small kitchen where she finished putting the finishing touches on everything, until finally the two sides were placed into her mother's antique serving bowls and taken over to the table.

They sat on opposite sides, but the table was small enough that they didn't feel like they were worlds apart. He decided to take charge, picking up the carving knife and fork to serve them both a generous portion of roast. He was sure it was more than they were probably going to have in a single meal, but he was willing to bet that with the previously empty fridge, Chastity didn't have nearly enough protein in her diet.

Then there were the sides. He put generous portions of that on his plate too. He knew that many men and women were concerned with watching their middles, but he worked plenty of calories off on the ranch, and he thought that Chastity looked perfect the way she was.

He never really understood society's current obsession with forcing women to be as thin as they could possibly be. He liked it when there was a softness to the feminine form, when his rough, veiny hands could sink into a curve and feel just how different and beautiful it was from his own body.

Such thoughts instantly made his body react though, and he shoved them away. Now was not the time.

Ben reached across the table and held Chastity's hands while he said grace.

When they had said Amen, Chastity looked up into Ben's eyes. "I want you to know that I really appreciate everything you've done for us. Especially considering..."

"Our history," he finished for her.

"Yeah, that."

"You don't have to thank me for everything. It's what good friends do for each other."

"Is that what we are?" she asked, looking across the table at him through her thick lashes. "Friends?"

He nodded, but then words were coming out of his mouth that he hadn't really intended to say. "I mean, you're the only friend that I want to kiss, but yes, I would consider us friends."

She blushed at that and took a bite of the food. He followed suit, and it gave them more time to think about what they were going to say. "I do like kissing you, still."

Oh.

That was interesting.

"I'm glad to hear it."

"Are you?"

"Yeah." He nodded, and his eyes focused in on her plush lips. "I am."

The conversation lapsed as they finished eating, but not from awkwardness. The food was even better than he had expected, and it was nice to just *be* in the moment.

Ben had never realized how he used his work on the ranch to fill every minute of his life, always keeping busy so that he would never feel lonely. Plus, it always ensured that he would drop into bed completely exhausted. Chastity brought so much more to his life, and he knew he would sorely miss her when she was gone.

Unless she didn't have to leave...

No, that was a dangerous line of thought, and he needed to leave it alone. He could cherish the time he had with Chastity, but that was it. To expect or want for more was only going to leave him heartbroken, and he'd had enough of that.

Eventually they both finished, and Chastity moved to take their dishes to the sink. He followed her, perhaps a little too closely, but the close proximity allowed him to smell her sweet vanilla bodywash and whatever magical concoction she used on her hair.

He brushed against her on accident as he placed his dishes in the sink, and the feel of her arm against his made his skin prickle. He wanted to reach out and pull her to him, to hold her so tightly to him that they fused into one. But instead, he leaned over and pressed a light kiss to her forehead.

She leaned into the gesture, her hands going to his chest where they rested, two points of heat against his torso. Once his lips pulled away, her face turned up to him, and he drank her features in like it was the first time he had ever seen her.

"You're beautiful, you know that, right?"

"No, but I feel that way when you look at me."

"Good. Then I should keep saying it."

"I wouldn't object."

Carefully, he lowered his arms to where they just rested on her wide hips, then pulled her to him until they were flush. Her body felt so right pressed against his, like they were made to be perfectly fitted puzzle pieces, and for a moment, he rested his head on top of hers.

They stood like that for several moments, rocking gently to an inaudible music that they seemed to feel more than hear.

"I miss this," she murmured into his chest, her voice a gentle and soothing vibration against his skin. "Being held by you."

"I miss holding you."

She hummed a murmur of agreement and tilted her head up once more, which made him lift his chin from her hair. They looked at each other again, and he was overwhelmed with the urge to kiss her.

But why even resist? They were two adults on a date. Surely a little kiss wouldn't be too inappropriate.

He ducked his lips down, his eyes half-lidded with his own want, and he felt her push up on her tip toes, he drew in a breath, wanting nothing more than to crash his mouth to hers once again. His heart leapt into his mouth and his whole body ached for her.

"Chastity, the nurse texted me and said she won't be able to make it tonight, but she can get us a replacement. Do you want that or can we just—" Mrs. Parker stood on the stairs and seemed genuinely surprised by his presence. "Oh, I didn't know you had company."

For the second time in a row, Ben found the romantic rise cut off by Chastity's mother.

Oh goodness.

20

Chastity

*I*t took all of the willpower in Chastity's body not to turn around and snap at her mother. But she knew her mom didn't mean to interrupt. She just had the uncanny timing of a Catholic school nun who wanted to make sure that nothing was going on between anyone.

"Hi, Mom," she said, turning. "I told you that Ben was coming over for a visit, remember? You said you'd be up reading to give us some space?"

"Oh... I don't recall that. But anyways, what do you want me to tell the nurse?"

Chastity looked to Ben, feeling a bit guilty again, but he smiled. "Take care of your mother," he whispered, lightly enough so that her mother couldn't hear.

"Tell her we don't need a replacement. You can hang out with us tonight."

"That sounds like fun!" Her eyes flicked to the dining room table and she clapped her hands. "Oh, is this what I've been smelling? You wouldn't mind if I helped myself, would you?"

"Of course not. And do you mind if Ben and I have dessert while you eat your dinner? Since we've already eaten."

"That sounds perfect, actually. It'll be like a real family meal together. Like before..." she cut herself off again in that telltale way she had been doing for the past month. "Like before," she finished without adding anything else.

"Yeah, that does sound nice. Why don't you have a seat, Mom, and I'll get you a plate."

Chastity's mom nodded and made her way to one of the unoccupied places. She sat down and texted the nurse. Chastity rushed to get her a plate and silverware before worrying about the dessert she had made.

As Chastity returned to the kitchen to get the desserts ready, her phone vibrated. She glanced over at where she'd put it on the counter. Her stomach lurched with excitement when she realized it was a text from her agent.

You got a callback!! Second auditions are next week. What day can you be back? I'll set it up.

Her hands were shaking. A callback. This was the break she'd been waiting for to get out of her slump. She started to text her agent back that she'd make any time work, then stopped. Any time would not work. She wasn't in New York. She was miles and miles away stuck in Blanche Creek. Taking care of her mother who couldn't be left alone. Having dinner with the man who made her heart race.

Life wasn't fair. Not at all.

She was going to have to think hard about this decision. She texted her agent. *Exciting! I'll let you know tomorrow.*

Chastity brought out the desserts she had made. In addition to the huckleberry pie, she had also made a mousse. Hazelnut and dark chocolate, and she was quite proud of it. It had taken quite a bit of work and even more clean up afterward.

But how big of an accomplishment was it compared to getting a part in a show? Despite being distracted, she tried to put on a happy face.

"That looks amazing," Ben said, as she served him a bowl back at his seat.

"It does, doesn't it?" her mother added, looking over from her plate. "I can't wait to try some once I get through dinner." She took a large bite of the roast Ben had placed on her plate while Chastity had been busy in the kitchen. "Oh goodness, but this is certainly delicious too."

"I'm glad you think so," Chastity said, sitting back in her spot. "I had fun cooking it."

While she still somewhat felt like kicking her mother for her poor timing, she did indeed love seeing her look so happy. That almost made up for not being able to kiss Ben like she really wanted to.

Almost.

"Goodness, Chastity, I should have you cook more often," her mother continued after a few minutes pause to eat the fare she had made. "Maybe it's a good thing your career failed in New York, so you can come here and feed me."

Chastity paused in bringing her spoon up to her mouth. "It didn't *fail*," she said adamantly, despite having thought that very same thing several times to herself. But the text from her agent had given her hope. "I was just in a bit of a slump. I have plenty lined up for me when I get home."

"Do you?" Ben asked, sounding surprised. "I thought it was going to be a bit until you returned."

"Well yeah, but that doesn't mean I don't want to go home soon."

"Wait, so you're abandoning me?" her mother asked, completely shocking her out of her good mood. "Why even stay here at all?"

"*Mom*, you always knew I was returning to New York. You too, Ben. I don't know why either of you are acting surprised."

"I'm not surprised," Ben said slowly, as if he was trying to contain his seething emotion. "I just thought you'd be here for a few more months."

"I sure hope I'm not," she blurted out before she could think better of it.

His face sharpened instantly. "What? Is staying here so painful for you? Are you so eager to run away that you'll do it the first chance you get?"

"Why are you acting this way?" Chastity found her voice rising. "You said you understood."

"Yeah, I understand," he said. "But I thought that you were going to take your time and go when everything was taken care of here. I thought we had *time*. I thought—" He cut himself off, shaking his head. "What are we even doing?"

"We're enjoying each other's company. Why think any more about it?"

"We should think more about it because I'm falling in love with you all over again. And I thought you were feeling the same way about me."

Her eyes went wide at the confession, and she felt such a strange mix of emotion within her that she could only stare at him for several moments. Guilt, affection, then anger, white-hot and choking.

Suddenly she was on her feet, and she didn't quite understand how she got there. "Why is that my fault? I've been nothing but honest with you. I can't stay here. The locals don't treat me like I belong, and every time they look at me, I feel this overwhelming need to prove to them that I'm so much more than what they think I am.

"You said you understood. You held me in your arms and looked at me with those sharp, green eyes and promised me that you got it. And now you want to be mad at me for doing exactly what I told you I was going to do?"

Now he was on his feet too. But he wasn't looming over her, threateningly like some men liked to do in an argument. Instead, he paced, running his hands through his sandy-blond hair. "Look, it's not that you're leaving. I get that this place isn't for you. I get that I'm not enough. But to hear you talk about leaving as if being here with me, with your mother, is painful to you—that hurts. You have to understand that, right? Are we so repugnant to you that you have to run away at top speed?"

Chastity stared at him in shock. "Why would you ever take it that way? This whole meal was to show you how grateful I am for everything you've done."

"You say that, but the look on your face just now when you reacted to staying for a few more months, that told me everything I need to know." He looked to her mother, his face struggling to remain stern and not enraged. "Mrs. Parker, I apologize for my behavior. I'll be going now. You have a good night."

"Oh dear, did I say something wrong?" she asked, looking between them with the most confused look on her expression.

"Not now, Mom," Chastity tried to say as lightly as she could before turning to Ben. "You walk out that door, and you will never see me again. We did this once, but we don't have to do it again. I've been upfront with you this entire time, so you have no reason to be mad like this."

Ben looked at her, and she could see emotions rushing

across his face. An eternity seemed to pass between them before his uncertain face hardened—and he walked right out the door.

Chastity watched him, mouth agape, and heard his truck door slam before his engine rumbled off. She ran to the still-open door and slammed it closed before sliding to the ground in a heap.

She couldn't help it—as she sat there, big, angry tears rolled down her cheeks. She hadn't cried in so long, refusing to let herself give in, and now she found herself sobbing and hiccupping in a real mess.

"Honey, what happened? I'm so confused."

Chastity heard her mother stand up and wobble over to her, but she couldn't reply right away. All the stress and uncertainly and now anger were flooding most of her brain, nearly drowning her in her tears. She had known that getting close to Ben was a stupid idea, but she had never imagined that it would crumble so easily. Perhaps it was foolish, but she thought maybe they could part with the bittersweet sting of love lost rather than clashing like two roiling clouds in a storm.

Dang it, she was such a fool. She wanted to shake her fist at the sky and ask him why he kept doing these kinds of things to her. Once more, she felt her barely rebuilt heart shattering to pieces inside her chest, only leaving bitter shards behind.

There was a thunk, and Chastity realized it was her mother planting her butt against the door, so she could slide down to sit next to her. Chastity looked at her, questions in her teary eyes.

"Did I do something wrong?"

For a moment, Chastity wanted to scream at her that *yes!* she did. She wanted to tell her mom that her career hadn't failed, and that she was going to make something of herself. That if maybe she and Dad hadn't been so insistent that all she could do was marry and have babies that she wouldn't be so set on breaking that mold.

But she couldn't say any of that, because it wasn't her full cognizant mother staring at her. No, Mrs. Ruby Parker was very sick, and this wasn't the time to air out old grudges.

"No, Mom, you didn't do anything wrong."

"Okay, dear."

She looped her skinny arm around Chastity's shoulders, and the two sat there while the younger Parker cried out all the pain filling her.

What was Chastity going to do?

21

Ben

*B*en threw a small hay bale from the top loft of the main barn down to the floor below. He tossed it a bit harder than he should have, and he heard Benji let out a colorful swear below him.

"Whoa, you okay up there?" he asked.

Ben didn't answer, and thankfully, his brother knew well enough to leave him alone with his thoughts. His next brother in line, however, was not so gracious.

"Hey, Ben, any reason why you're trying to kill us down here?" Bart's voice had that edge to it of barely restrained anger. He had been struggling with that a lot since he came back, but he had been doing better in the most recent weeks. It all seemed to depend on whether he was having his night terrors or not.

But still, Ben grated at Bart's words. He didn't feel like talk-

ing. He didn't feel like explaining. The only thing he felt like
was an idiot.

He *knew* that Chastity was leaving. He even got it, on some
level in his brain. But when he had seen her react to the idea of
staying for a couple more months, like it was some awful
torture that she had to endure, it had cut him right down to his
core.

"Maybe if you all worked a little faster, you wouldn't be in
the way now," he snapped.

"Wow. Cranky."

"Leave him be," Benji hissed loud enough for Ben to catch
his words. "It's obvious he's having a hard time with
something."

"Yeah, but I'm just saying, shouldn't we try to help our
brother out if he's hurting? Isn't that what you lot are always
tellin' me? That we're all here for each other?"

Ben sighed. He and his brothers had always been close,
especially when one of them was hurt, but he preferred that
kind of attention go to Bart, or Bryant, the two who really
needed it—although for vastly different reasons.

"Look," Ben said, leaning over the loft. But before he could
get any farther, a loud whoop echoed through the space, star-
tling the few animals that had chosen to linger around rather
than go frolic in the fields.

His head turned toward the entrance to see an almost unfamiliar shape; that's how rarely his youngest brother visited
from the nearby city.

"What's up, losers?" Bryant asked, lifting his hands in the air
like he was at some sort of concert.

"Oh, Bryant, it's you," Bart said, sounding absolutely unen-
thused. "To what do we owe this visit?"

"Whoa, Bartie-boy. Surprised to see you up and about. The bombs not going off in your head anymore?"

Bart was quiet a moment, and Ben felt his anger spike. Trust Bryant to rile up what didn't need to be riled. Clambering down the ladder, Ben arrived in the group of Miller boys just as Bart found his words.

"I'm going to the main house to see if Mother needs anything," he said, striding off and not so kindly knocking into the youngest brother's shoulder with his own.

"Geez," Bryant said, rolling his eyes. "What crawled up his butt?"

"Do you always have to be such a jerk?" Benji asked in exasperation.

"*What*? He's been back for almost a year. Are we still to the point where we can't joke about it?"

"PTSD is a serious illness. We may never be able to joke about it," Ben said evenly. He was disappointed in his youngest brother, but unsurprised.

Being the littlest out of five had resulted in Bryant Miller being spoiled, and he was the only one that Ben would consider the leach of the family. He spent almost all of his time in bars and hotels of the surrounding area, sleeping with whatever young women caught his fancy, and spending tons of his parents' money. Ben shuddered to think at how much money he had blown at the casinos and didn't understand why Ma and Pa didn't cut him off.

But they would just wax on and off about the prodigal son and how he would soon return to ranch life. Ben was not so certain.

"Ugh. How boring. This is why I don't come around here anymore. You lot are always so depressing."

"So why *are* you here?" Benji asked, a sigh implicit in his words.

"I wanted to check on my biggest bro," Bryant said, smirking like he was oh-so-clever. "I hear that big ol' Ben is chasing after the same ex that broke his heart all those years ago and made him turn against women."

Ben paled at that. He hated being the talk of the town, and if there were already rumors going about...he hated to think about it.

"I haven't turned against women," he objected, trying to avoid the rest of what he said altogether.

"Sure, whatever you say. But that's not what Madeline told me."

"Who is Madeline?" Benji asked.

"Oh, no one you know. But I think Benny-boy here is familiar with her brother."

Ben's patience was wearing thin. He loved his littlest brother, but he was a right pain most of the time. "What do you mean?"

"I think you got into a bit of a row with him. Apparently, her brother works for a bank in the city. Some girl hauled off and punched him, and I heard that you were the one who diffused the whole situation by flaunting our family name a little."

Ben instantly knew who he was talking about. "Well, tell Madeline that her brother is an absolute sleazeball."

"Oh, she knows about that. He's also got a big mouth on top of all the character flaws she blabbed on and on about for at least an hour."

For the second time, Ben found he was having to repeat himself, but with far less patience. "What do you mean?"

"Apparently your long-lost love's not gonna be around for much longer."

"Yeah, I know that—"

"No, you don't, big guy, so don't interrupt me. Because if you did know, you'd have that look on your face when you think justice isn't being done. She's not gonna be gone because she's smart enough to leave this awful town, but because their house is on its way to repossession in a couple of months. Madeline's brother is doing what he can to stop the process, but they're so behind on their mortgage that the minimum payments they are making are only adding days to the cutoff point rather than helping much."

"Wait, what?" Ben said, the conversation going nowhere near where he thought it was.

"Whoa, repossessed?" Benji added.

Bryant nodded. "Yeah. It's a sad thing, actually. The mom's sick, I hear, and will probably be shipped off to one of those state-run nursing homes—and you know how those are. My money is that your girl will try to move close to the nursing home, so she can keep an eye on them and make sure no one is abusing her mom, but Madeline bets she'll run right back to the big city and never look back here."

Ben stared at him, shocked and trying to figure out which emotions he was going to pay attention to. There were a lot going through him, and he wasn't sure what to do with that much input from his brain.

"*There* it is," Bryant said, clapping his hands. "That's the look I was talking about."

Benji didn't seem to appreciate his tone. "You know, I'm starting to think that you came here to tell us this, so you could gloat, rather than actually help your brother."

Bryant shrugged. "Think that if you want. I knew he would probably want to know what was going on with his short, curvy, and beautiful not-girlfriend. Forgive me for enjoying the fact that he wears his emotions like a comic book character."

"It's fine," Ben said, still sorting his thoughts. "Thank you for telling me, Bryant. Maybe you'll want to stick around for dinner? I know Mother would love to see you."

"Eh, I would, but there's this massive party at all the frat houses in the city, and I'm not gonna miss that."

"Aren't you a little old to be going to college parties?" Benji said, still clearly irritated.

"You're never too old to have fun, and all the college hunnies are—"

"*Thank you*, Bryant," Ben said firmly. "I'm sure dinner will be done in time for you to go and flirt with women who are too young for you. It really would make Mother happy."

"I'll think about it, I guess. It has been a while since I've had a good, homecooked meal."

"Thanks." Ben looked to his two brothers, suddenly quite exhausted. "Hey, Benji, do you mind taking over? I think I'm gonna go take a break."

"Yeah, of course," Benji said. "You never take breaks as it is. Make sure you help yourself to some water."

"Will do."

Ben strode to the main house in silence, completely in his head as his legs moved on their own. He was shocked at the revelation. Did Chastity know? She had to know.

Was that why she was so eager to go back to New York? When he had taken her mother to the doctor, she had gone on and on about how hard-working Chastity was and how she went to the library every day to earn money on the internet and wrote articles well into the night. Obviously, she couldn't get a regular job because she needed to watch her mother, but she was still trying to make a buck.

That kind of stress had to be awful. No wonder she wanted to get out of town. But still... she could have asked for help. He'd be happy to lend a hand, whatever she needed.

Actually... could she have asked for help?

She had always been the independent sort, if anything was proven by her decade in the big city. On top of that, she had only just started trusting him again, and he had ruined that by getting into a fight with her on their second date.

It was so frustrating. He was such an idiot! But still, it wasn't wrong of him to have been so hurt by her anxiousness to get away when she hadn't told him the whole story, was it? Or had he been subconsciously upset that he wasn't enough for her and looking for any excuse to get into an argument?

Ben reached his room and sat on his bed for a moment, grateful that he hadn't run into any more of his family members. Thoughts and feelings swirled in his brain. Part of him was whispering that this wasn't his responsibility and he needed to keep his nose out of it. But it was a tiny part. The rest was clamoring somewhere between anger, indignance, and guilt. Even if he was mad at Chastity, even if he was hurt by her, even if he was certain that he would never love anyone again like he loved her, he still wanted what was best for her.

Even if that wasn't him.

Rising from the bed, he went back down the hall toward the main house. There he saw Ma had come in from the chicken coop, two daughters of one of their workers clinging to her apron as she explained how to wash the eggs.

"Hey Ma, can I talk to you a minute?"

His mom looked up, a smile across her face before she noticed Ben's expression. "Yes, dear. Just one moment." She set the eggs carefully to the side and dismissed the children, who scampered off out the door to one of the many cabins at the edge of the cattle fields. He wasn't sure whose daughters they were as he rarely hung around the children, but the Miller Ranch had been lucky enough to have the same families of workers with them for generations. Apparently, it started out with a mute guy years ago, who was some long-lost son of a tycoon.

But that was a story for another day. For now, what was important was Chastity.

"What's wrong, dear?" Ma asked, taking his arm and gently leading him to the couch. "You've got that look on your face."

Ben let out a bitter chuckle. "You're the second one to point out my looks. It must be a thing."

"But that's not what's bothering you."

"No. It isn't." He sat there a moment, collecting his thoughts. Speaking without thinking was partially what had gotten him into this mess. "Chastity and I got into a fight."

"Ah, I am not surprised at that," she said with a nod. "You're both so strong-willed, and you want such opposite things."

"If you knew, then why did you encourage things between us?"

"Did I?" Ma asked. "Perhaps I still held onto hope that the two of you might find common ground. It's strange, the two of you seem so meant for each other, but every time you get close, something pushes you apart."

"Yeah, something like that."

"But I trust that you didn't need to talk to me about the fight," her wise, kind eyes regarded him as only a mother could. "There's something else."

It probably should have been nerve wracking for her to read through him so thoroughly, but he was used to it after thirty years. "There is. I found out today that her house is probably getting repossessed. I want to do something, but I might have ruined the only chance I had of Chastity trusting me."

"So, you want my advice?"

Ben nodded, looking to her hopefully. While he loved his father dearly, he had always been much closer to his mother. She was so wise, and rarely judged him, even when he was losing his head over a woman he'd been parted from for a decade.

"Then I'm going to tell you honestly, that I don't know."

"You don't... know?"

That seemed like an impossible sentence out of her mouth. Ma not knowing? But Ma knew everything, even the things that he didn't want her to. "What do you mean?" It felt like he'd been saying that a lot that day, but he wouldn't have to if the world would start making sense.

"I mean, I don't know. I can see reasons to help her, and reasons not to. You could infringe on her privacy and pride by inserting yourself into a situation she never asked you to. But on the other hand, you could also take a tremendous load of stress from her. Potentially turn their financial situation around."

"You're reiterating everything that's been going through my mind. Every time I think of a positive, I come up with a negative and vice versa."

She nodded gravely, and he appreciated that she was taking the situation seriously and not just telling him to get a grip. "For probably the first time in my memory, I don't have advice for you. So, I think you should take it a step higher."

"What? Father?" Ben asked. "You know he's not really one for these sorts of things."

She laughed at that. "I more meant *the* Father. I think you should pray on it. Ask the Lord if you're troubled."

"I'm not sure if that would help in this situation."

"I've found that it can often help in any situation." Her wrinkled hand alighted on his shoulder. "I know that we don't always get answers back that we understand, but sometimes even just vocalizing what's troubling you and the choices you have can help your mind figure out what's best for you." She squeezed his shoulder—her farmer's wife hands still strong.

"Just give it a try, if you can," she added.

Ben nodded, less than satisfied with that answer, but still appreciating that his mother genuinely was trying to help. He could always count on her.

It was too bad that Chastity didn't have that same comfort. Between the friction with her mother, and then Mrs. Parker's illness, there wasn't exactly a ton of room for comfort and validation.

Why couldn't he be this understanding of her situation all the time? It wasn't often that his temper got the better of him, but this entire situation could have been avoided if he hadn't lost his cool at the dinner a few nights ago.

Back to his bachelor addition and in his large, familiar room, Ben found himself pacing, his mother's words replaying in his head. He supposed some prayer couldn't hurt, so he went to grab his Bible.

Maybe his mother was right. Even if God didn't want to end up involved in his dramatic romance, maybe just vocalizing things would help.

But as he went to sit, a picture fell to the floor. Bending over, he picked it up and a strange tremor went through his hand as he realized the moment it was capturing.

It was Chastity and him, after a summer camp that they had both volunteered at that introduced inner city kids to animals and rural activities. They were arm in arm, both brilliantly tanned from being outside, and smiling like absolute doofuses.

Ben's fingers traced the memory, remembering how happy he was then and how it seemed like they could take on anything. Chastity used to confide everything in him, and he was her rock. She could have survived without him, but he liked to think that he had saved her at least some hassle.

Turning the photo over and over again in his hands, he wondered just what he was supposed to do, and if he could ever get her to smile like that again.

Or had he ruined everything?

22

Chastity

*C*hastity finished up her article, saving it to her folder for her trip to the library the next day. Unfortunately, on Sunday the library was closed, meaning she wasn't going to be uploading anything today.

She sipped at her tea, her stomach churning too much for breakfast. Thankfully, her mother was still asleep and unable to lecture her on her bad habit of skipping "the most important meal of the day."

Chastity sighed, rubbing her nose as she tried to think of the next article she hoped to squeeze in before her mother awoke and started shuffling around. In the two weeks that she had been writing articles and filling out surveys, she'd actually managed to rack up half a grand. It wasn't nearly enough to put a dent in her parents' debt, but she was pleasantly surprised at how well her articles were doing on a consistent basis. She was only another five hundred dollars away from hitting the next level of authorization, where she would be paid more per article and be assigned to more clients. If she really pushed herself, maybe she could do that in another week.

After all, it wasn't like she had anything else to do. Whatever had been happening between her and Ben was well and truly over, even if it left a gnawing pain in her middle.

Was she wrong for how she had reacted? She certainly hadn't meant anything by her visceral response at the thought of being stuck in this town for another three months, babysitting her mother and barely scraping by, trying to ration out the food his family had given her to last as long as possible. But the stress was getting to her. While she knew she very well might end up stuck here for three more months, thinking about it made her want to cry, pull her hair out, and lie down for an exceedingly long nap.

And she'd had to text her agent, telling him she couldn't come back to New York yet. Giving up the chance for the callback that could have been her big break. Chastity had decided her mom needed her more than she needed that part.

But he didn't know all that. From what her mother had told her, he seemed to think that they didn't have groceries because she was too busy to go and buy them then walk back to the house every day, not because they literally had no money. And Chastity didn't really want to tell him about their financial situation.

Far too many people tried to use the Millers for their money, and she wouldn't be one of them. Sure, if it came down to her mother's health, she would ultimately ask them, but she wanted to try her hardest to do this herself.

Besides, if she was already doing this well with the whole

article-writing gig, maybe she could expand that even more in the coming months.

She could only hope.

Shoving the rest of her feelings down, Chastity focused on her article. She only got about halfway through before she heard footsteps down the stairs. Looking up, she saw her mother standing there, dressed up in her Sunday best.

"Are you ready for church, dear?"

Chastity blinked at her, an internal sigh building in her chest. She hadn't been able to take her mother to church on Wednesday either, and she was sure the woman was going to be extra insistent now.

"I'm sorry, Mom, but I really have to finish about five more articles, so I have enough for when the next wave of bills comes." The site that she used held onto the money she made for about a week, so it definitely required specific planning to make sure she had the money when she needed it. "Can we go next week?"

"You said that last week."

"I know, I know. But there's a lot of catching up to do."

"Certainly, a couple of hours won't stop you from doing that."

"It really could, Mom. I'm burning the candles at both ends here."

Her mother stared at her, dark eyes intense, before her jaw set in a firm way. "Fine, then I will go myself. I'll make sure to pray for you, as well, that hopefully your deadlines will be finished on time, and that you'll come to church with me next time."

Now the suppressed sigh came out in full force. "Mom, I don't think it's very wise for you to go to the other edge of town by yourself. Especially considering how…"—she had to be careful how she mentioned her mother's sickness, because that seemed to be an especially potent trigger for her— "run down you've been lately."

"I'm not a child, Chastity." Ah, her favorite line. "I don't know why you insist on treating me that way."

"I'm not treating you like a child. I'm looking out for you."

"I don't need you to watch out for me!" Her face reddened, and she actually stomped her foot. "You're being ridiculous, Maggie!"

Ah, Maggie. Her mother's older sister, who had passed away from cancer before Chastity was even born. That was a new one.

"Mom—"

"Look, I'm going to church. All right? You can't stop me!"

Why did everything have to resort to shouting lately, rubbing her temples, Chastity felt herself want to sink into the floor. "Mom, I promise that I'll take you to church next week. Please, just work with me here."

"No! You don't get to treat me like this just because you're the eldest! I'm going."

She stormed toward the door, and Chastity knew that she couldn't let her go out in this state. She would get lost, and wander, and heaven forbid end up somewhere dangerous.

Jumping to her feet, Chastity stood in the doorway, blocking her path. Her mother glared her down, but she just returned it.

"Mom, stop. Please, be reasonable for once."

"I *am* reasonable, Maggie!"

"For God's sake, I'm *not* Maggie!" Chastity snapped. "I'm your *daughter*. I'm your daughter, and I'm trying to take care of you while the doctors figure out what's going on, okay? You're sick, Mom. You're sick, and you need to accept that, okay?"

"I'm not sick! I'm fine. I'm *fine!*"

Her palms reached out smacking against Chastity's shoulders. It didn't hurt, but it was shocking to have her mother strike her. In all her years, she'd never so much as spanked her, preferring punishment that actually worked on her strong-willed child.

"Let me go. *Let me go!*"

"I can't," Chastity said, taking the multiple hits. What did she do in this situation? Why did everything have to be so *hard*? She just wanted her mother back. Was that too much to ask?

Her mother's anger quickly transitioned into tears, and soon she was sobbing as her hands went between clutching Chastity's clothes to striking her more. It didn't take long for her to lose her energy, and her hands fell to her sides and she slumped against her daughter.

"I'm sorry, Mom," Chastity said, wrapping her arms around her mother. She felt so guilty. She was treating her mother like some prisoner under house arrest, but she didn't know what else to do. If she took the time to take her mother out and let her visit every place she wanted, they'd never get out of the hole her parents had dug themselves into. "I really am."

"Nothing makes sense, Maggie. Nothing. Every time I think I have my feet under me, they're ripped away and I'm falling again."

She cried against Chastity's chest, no more words to her plea, and Chastity knew what she had to do.

"Hey, Mom?"

"Yes?" Did she know who Chastity was now? She seemed to have calmed a bit, but that would make this a short episode and mostly hers lasted for hours.

"Would you like to go to church?"

She wiped her face, hiccuping slightly before giving a slow nod. "Yes. I would like to do that very much."

"All right. How about we stand up, wash our faces, and then go? Do you think we'll still make it in time?"

"I believe so," she said, wiping her face with her sleeve.

"Then that's the plan. Come on now, on our feet."

They both stumbled upright, and Chastity went about packing some things, so they could go. She had made a lot of mistakes with her mother, mostly because she had no idea what she was doing, but she was trying her best.

And sometimes trying her best meant making up for lost time.

23

Ben

*B*en got off the phone with a sigh, flopping back onto his bed and staring at the ceiling as if the answer for all that he was looking for was written up there. He had reached a decision, but he had no idea if he was doing the right thing.

A lightbulb flashed in the corner of his room, which meant someone was ringing the bell at the end of the hall leading into his bachelor's attachment.

He briefly thought about ignoring it, but his family generally left him alone when he was in his home, which meant that it was probably urgent.

He groaned and got to his feet, heading out of his room and toward the door at the end of the short hall separating him from the main house. He opened the door and was surprised to see his mother there—love and concern clear across her features.

"Hello, son."

"Hello there, Ma. Do you need something?"

"I just wanted to know if you talked with God, and how it went."

"Ah..." he let the silence linger for several moments while he decided what he wanted to say—if anything. "I did something."

"Something like..."

He shrugged. "I don't want to talk about it. I'm still not sure if it was the right call."

"What makes you think that?"

"Because I feel like I'm not certain of anything anymore. I'm in love with a woman who I would have told you was the devil for the past ten years, and I understand that she has to leave, but at the same time I hate it more than anything else. It's incredibly dramatic and confusing, and I miss when I didn't need anyone but us."

"Would you come with me for a minute?" his mother said softly, without judgment as she held out her hand.

"Why?"

"There's something I want to tell you. It just came to mind, and I think it might be helpful to you."

"All right then, I guess I don't have anything to do but the chores."

She grabbed his hand and led him back to the living room and toward her favorite sitting couch. "Have I ever told you the story of your great-great-great-grand-uncle who married into our family after kicking his betrothed to the curb?"

"Uh, no. I don't even know how many years ago that many greats takes us."

"Fair enough. But this was back with the second generation. You and your brother recently cleared out the grove he planted for her as a wedding present, actually."

"You mean Juniper's Grove?"

She nodded. "Juniper was the youngest daughter of the Millers and quite independent. Since she was the baby, her parents weren't eager to marry her off and let her help her brothers how she wished. Eventually, a runaway horse helped introduce her to the town butcher, who was the son of the previous butcher."

"And what, they fell madly in love and she realized that love was all right, and you think Chastity will do that if I find a runaway horse?"

Ma laughed lightly, patting his shoulder. "Hardly. As I mentioned earlier, there was a betrothed to worry about. She was a mail-order bride from back East and apparently she was right awful."

"Uh-huh."

"She hated children; she hated the West; and she hated that her husband wasn't super rich."

"Sounds like a real catch."

"Oh, she was. Especially since her soon-to-be husband, your uncle, was raising his two siblings, after their mother had passed away.

"He tried to endure her—he really did. But she was volatile and even hit him in front of Juniper and her family. So eventually, he knew that he had to break it off with her.

"It wasn't easy. He knew that refusing her outright would risk her rage, plus repercussions from her family, who had paid him quite the handsome dowry to be rid of her. One day they were stranded at the side of the road when a rich merchant's son passed by. After seeing the man, an idea popped into his head, and he seized it with both hands.

"Little more than a few days later, the betrothed left him for the richer man, and he was able to then date Juniper without losing out on the dowry."

"So, are you trying to tell me that I can have my cake and eat it too? I'm not sure I'm quite catching the moral here."

"I'm just saying, that our ancestors have been in seemingly impossible social situations as well, yet somehow it all worked out. I won't say that it was easy, or painless, but in the end, everyone was happy."

"So you're saying that I should try to foist Chastity off on someone even richer than us," he retorted, this time more teasingly than his first question.

She tsked her tongued and gently swatted his arm. "You think you're so smart, don't you? Just like your father. All I want you to know is that it's important you at least try something, and as far as you know, it might work out."

"Yeah, maybe." And yet his mood was lifted, and he felt ready to get back to work. If anything, he liked work because it kept him from overthinking everything like Chastity tended to.

"I think I'm going to head out. Thank you, Ma."

"You're welcome, son."

Ben leaned over to give her a kiss on the cheek and headed out the door. But before he could exit, he heard his mother call out to him.

"Dear?"

"Yes?"

"Are you going to call Chastity and talk to her?"

Ben paused in his exit, having not even thought about it before. "I think not. The way I see it, one of two things will happen. Either she'll forgive me and stay, or she'll go back to New York where she can live out her *dreams*."

"Are you really going to let her go like that again?"

Ben shrugged. "Like you said, sometimes things work out. Sometimes they don't. I guess we'll have to wait and see."

"You have such a funny way of listening to me."

He grinned at her, feeling cheeky, as he often called Chastity. "But at least I listen. It's more than you can say for some of my other brothers."

Her eyes narrowed. "You've been talking to Bryant again, haven't you?"

"How did you know?" Ben said with a laugh before heading out the door.

The route ahead wasn't clear, and he had a feeling that he might end up as alone as he had been for the past ten years.

But at least he could say that he tried.

And he supposed that was the best he could do.

24

Chastity

*C*hastity didn't know why she felt nervous as she approached the large spire of the town church. She had visited this place hundreds of times during her younger years and had never felt out of place before.

But now, as she looked at the other churchgoers who were taking their places, she felt like she didn't belong.

She did believe in God, mostly. But he was more of a something that hung in the back of her mind rather than directing her whole life. She was sure her mother would have an apoplexy if she ever spoke those words out loud.

Speaking of her mother, she glanced over at her as they gently marched forward. For the first half of the short walk, she had still been shaking slightly and red faced, often needing to blow her nose, but now that they were reaching the end, she seemed to be much more recovered.

In fact, she was standing straight, and a serene expression was across her face. Chastity felt another wave of guilt that she had delayed this for so long when obviously it meant quite a lot to her mother.

But what was done was done, and there was no changing the past, as much as she liked to overanalyze, overthink, and overwork it. Chastity focused on making this trip everything her mother needed.

They went inside the door, and Chastity was almost dunked—head first—into nostalgia.

The church, not ever having central air installed, still had the same massive black fan pointed at the entrance, and then another pointing at the congregation. The low hum tickled up her spine, and she remembered how when she was a child, she would talk into the blades to have it make her voice sound robotic.

She allowed her mom to pull her toward the front, past the final pews for latecomers and more toward the center pews. Chastity's face burned at that, but she didn't object. If her mom wanted to sit in the center pews, then they would sit in the center pews.

Eventually, she did find an open spot and slid in, Chastity following her. It seemed that they had only missed the opening announcements, statements, and prayer. The congregation hadn't even gone into worship yet.

Chastity had always loved that part. She wasn't the best singer, but it was always nice to vocalize, and the congregation was loud enough that she didn't have to worry about hitting a wrong note or two.

Sure enough, the band started up eventually, the guitarists and bassist plucking away while the pianist tried to go old-fashioned on the keys. And yet somehow, it worked.

Worship flew by in a blur, and Chastity didn't find herself nearly as bored with the sermon as she had as a teenager. She remembered how often she had wanted to sleep in, and slightly resented the reverend for having a voice akin to a very low lullaby. But there was a new reverend now, and he was a bit livelier, so maybe that was the difference.

All too soon, however, it started to wind down, the ushers having come to collect a tithe that Chastity didn't have, and it was time for the final prayer. She had been content to sit in the pew with her head bowed, but her mother was on her feet like it was a race, gunning it for the kneeling bench at the front of the church. What was that called? The altar? She didn't know. It had been a long time since she had gone to church.

But she wasn't going to let her mother kneel there alone, so she followed after her.

For a moment, she felt like all the eyes in church were on her, even though she knew that was incredibly unlikely. Somehow, she made it to the front without chickening out, and she knelt next to her mother—who immediately bowed her head.

Chastity followed her example, not wanting to stick out any more than she did already. She tried to think of a general prayer to look more of the part, but soon she heard her mother muttering and that caught all of her attention.

"Lord, please, I need you. I need you so terribly." Her mom's voice caught as she prayed, making Chastity's heart ache. Did her mother realize she could hear her? Did it matter? "It feels like my world is crumbling all around me, and I don't know what to do. A lot of times my head is muddy, and I feel like I'm losing whole days."

She continued on, and every word out of her mouth made Chastity ache. Chastity had thought maybe her mother didn't know the situation that well, that her sickness kept her in her own protective bubble. Apparently, that wasn't the case.

"I miss Charlie so much, Lord. I know you bring us to you when the time is right, but the world doesn't seem possible without him. It's like someone stole all the color from my sunrise. Or snatched away all of the beautiful music that ever existed. I feel empty, Lord. Empty, and alone, and confused.

"Please, I beg of you. I need your guidance in these times. I need the peace that I used to feel all the time in you. It feels like my heart is gone and every single breath pains me deep in my soul."

Tears welled up in Chastity's eyes, and she was doing her best to stop it, lest she break her mother's concentration. But it was difficult. Guilt mixed with empathy, mixed with the rampant desire to *do something*, but having no idea what to do.

It wasn't fair. She'd been thinking that far too much lately, but it was true! Her mother tried to live right her whole life, always loving the Lord, always trying to do her best by people— even if her and Chastity had fought often about their stances on certain issues. She had been kind, and loving, and yet here she was, wasting away of a broken heart and mind.

To stand by and watch was excruciating. Chastity wanted to do something, but they hadn't even received the test results yet from the last round of doctor visits when her mom had gone with Ben. If only—

Thinking his name sparked something in her, and suddenly realization snapped through her mind so fast she nearly got whiplash.

"Dear God," she whispered to herself.

Her mind was spinning out into the stratosphere.

Because suddenly, she understood Ben.

Sure, he *was* the one who had broken his promise to go with her. Sure, he was the one that flipped out at dinner. But she finally understood the *why* of why he had reacted so viscerally.

He loved her, she had always known that, but he really, *genuinely* loved her, which was why he worked so hard to understand her too. But she kept abandoning him without a look over her shoulder. Chasing big dreams like he was some sort of afterthought.

And it wasn't that he wanted her to give up on them, or that it would be right for her to, it was just that he needed to see or hear that it was difficult for her to leave him. That it hurt her as much as it hurt him and that she cherished him as well. He could let her go, let her chase her big dreams. He just wanted to know that he still held a place in her heart underneath all of the independence.

He was afraid of being forgotten.

Deep down in his heart, he was afraid that he was going to be left behind, like her mother was now.

Oh goodness.

Shame poured down her soul, and she wondered how it could have taken her so long to get something so simple. He just wanted to know he mattered. That was it. Had she been so busy steeling herself against the rest of the world that she had forgotten how to empathize with the person that she had been closest to?

It seemed that way, which was certainly a shame.

But she could fix it, right? It wasn't too late. She was still in town, and so was he. Or had she ruined it all already? Would she ever be able to face him again after that terrible dinner? To go from nearly kissing to screaming in anger was not a pleasant transition in her book.

She didn't know, and she didn't come up with an answer as her mother continued to gently pray beside her. Chastity didn't even notice her mom was finished until she felt a gentle squeeze on her arm.

"I'm ready to go home now."

Chastity opened her eyes and looked around, surprised to see that it was only them and a couple of others left. Apparently, the service had concluded, and she hadn't even been aware.

"Do you need someone to pray with you?"

Chastity heard another unfamiliar and soft voice. Turning her head to the front, she saw a woman in a demure dress standing on the steps leading up to the main preaching area. She had a Bible in her hand, and her hair was pulled up into a sensible bun.

"Oh no, it's fine. We were just finishing up, actually."

"Are you certain?" she asked, smiling softly. She really was pretty, with golden skin and other features which made Chastity think she might have been part Asian. "I usually like to stay here for a while and fellowship, so it really wouldn't be any trouble."

"Thank you, Keiko," Chastity's mom said, slowly standing and bending her knees several times. "But I'm afraid I do get awful stiff after a while, and I'd like to go home and rest. It's been a... morning and a half, to put it lightly."

"I understand, Mrs. Parker." The woman's smile grew even softer, and Chastity wondered who this young lady was. "And you must be Chastity. I've heard so much about you."

"You have?"

She nodded, extending her hand for a shake. "Your parents used to come here all the time and were always early to my Bible study. If you ever need someone to talk to, I'm almost always here."

"Thank you. I appreciate that."

"Of course." She closed her eyes in a very cheek-filled grin before pulling her hand back. "Well, I suppose I should go take inventory of the food pantry for our next big delivery run. I hope to see the two of you another day." She gave a little bow of her head then wandered off.

Maybe Chastity didn't have to be as alone in this town as she thought.

"Are you ready, dear?" her mother asked, cutting into Chastity's introspection.

"Huh? Oh, yeah. I think I am." She offered her arm, and her mother took it.

Despite losing out on so much article time, Chastity was glad that she had done this. She felt like she'd had about a lifetime worth of epiphanies packed into a very short time and wanted to sort all of it out.

Maybe, just maybe, if she thought long and hard enough about it, she would find a way for her and Ben to, at the very least, be friends.

Wouldn't that be something?

25

Chastity

To say that the Parker routine changed slightly would be an understatement. A lot happened in the week following their fateful visit to church, and their lives seemed to be better for it.

They went back to the church every single day. Perhaps it was just psychosomatic, but Chastity felt like it was making a big difference already. Her mother's episodes were shorter, and she only had two in one week. Obviously, it was too soon to say anything definitive, but it certainly seemed like fellowship did indeed help strengthen her.

As for Chastity, well she did a range of things. It turned out the church had Wi-Fi, so she could submit her articles and finish a couple of surveys during Bible studies and other meetups that her mother went to. Of course, she paid attention in the Sunday service she attended, but she didn't think God would mind her still making money during their extracurricular visits.

Once Keiko had found out that she was working, she showed Chastity an office she could use while her mother was doing her thing. Chastity was incredibly grateful for it and promised Keiko that they'd have to go out sometime together and enjoy the town outside of the church.

If Chastity ever had the money to go out again.

All in all, things were steadily improving, and the world seemed less like a hopeless, black pit of despair that could never be escaped—which was exactly what Chastity needed.

But even with all those positives, guilt still weighed heavily on her heart about the whole Ben thing, and she dreaded running into a Miller. Although they both attended the same church, the Millers went to the much earlier service, while Chastity and her mother preferred the later one. That had kept them apart so far, but it was surely only a matter of time before their paths crossed again, and Chastity had no idea what she would say or do when it did.

Ben hadn't called or texted since the fight, which she took to mean that he was still mad and wanted nothing to do with her. She couldn't blame him, considering that she had made it seem like getting away from him and everything else in this small town was all she wanted. But that wasn't it at all. She just didn't want to be a failure, like she felt her mother and father had always inadvertently called her. She knew they never approved of her being an independent woman, being an actress and moving to the Big Apple. She had lumped Ben in with all of that mess as well, when that wasn't *quite* what was happening.

It seemed they both needed to work on their listening skills. Who knew the lesson could be so simple?

"Are you all right? You look like you're thinking some deep thoughts."

Chastity blinked, coming out of her inner monologue to remember that Keiko was leading her to the office again. It was Monday, which meant that it was the Christian support group for the widows in town. Although sad that there had to be such a thing, Chastity was glad there was that resource available for her mother. If she had known about the meetings earlier, she certainly would have gotten her mother there ASAP.

"Just thinking about life," Chastity answered vaguely as Keiko unlocked the door with her set of keys. Apparently, she was like the right-hand man to the reverend, although she wasn't related to him and wasn't looking to go into theology herself. She just really seemed to love the church and the townspeople. Chastity wished she had that kind of kindness in her.

"I see. Well, don't think too hard. I see a sort of brightness ahead for you, Chastity. I think good things are coming your way."

"Really?" she answered with a wry grin. "That would certainly be a nice change of pace."

"Well, it is what I've been praying for."

Chastity couldn't help but smile at that. There was such a genuine earnestness to Keiko. What wasn't there to love? How the girl wasn't snatched up and sporting a ring on her finger was beyond Chastity. "You've been praying for me?"

"Of course. I pray for all my friends."

"Oh, so we're friends now?"

Keiko's hazel eyes widened, as she gave her a surprised expression. "I had thought so. Was that too forward of me?"

"No, not at all. It's nice to hear it actually. Thank you, Keiko."

"You're welcome, friend. I'll see you in an hour or so?"

"Sounds good."

Chastity headed into the office and got settled, opening her laptop and checking her notifications on the article site. She always liked to check her milestones first, it was like getting a mini-payday every time she logged on.

Her eyes widened as she saw fifteen different messages she had waiting for her. The five-dollar milestone. The ten-dollar milestone. The twenty-dollar milestone. The *fifty*-dollar milestone!

She had a total of twenty-one articles up, and between them she had managed to earn a hundred dollars in a single day. What was going on?

She was nearly giddy as she went through them all, but she noticed she still had one more message from the admin in her inbox. Clicking on it, all color drained from her face and she didn't know whether to laugh or cry.

Dear Ms. Parker,

Due to your excellent, consistent work with our site, we wanted to extend you an offer to become a verified contributor. This is a full-time position, although there is the flexibility to set your own hours.

Please contact us at your earliest convenience with the best times to reach you to discuss the position.

Regards,

The Great Listicle Team

Chastity read it again. And then again.

She couldn't believe it.

They were offering her a *full-time job*?

Not only a job, but one as a verified contributor? That was huge! When she had first started with the site, she had read over their whole structure, and it was possible for the most popular of their writers to earn a grand or two a week.

Oh goodness.

The things she could do with that kind of money!

But she was getting ahead of herself. Quickly she sent off an email and gave them her cell phone number and let them know that she was only available for a phone call for the next couple of hours today. Then she finally allowed herself to jump out of her chair and squeal like a little school girl.

Oh goodness! She wanted to tell the entire world. She didn't know whether she should run out and find Keiko, or interrupt her mother's group, or call Ben, or *anything*! Her mind was an anxious, mixed-up batch of happiness, and it was so foreign that she wasn't sure how she was even going to function beyond the next breath.

But before she could figure any of that out, her phone rang. She took a deep breath before answering the unfamiliar number and managed not to sound insane when she answered.

"Hello?"

"Hello, is this Ms. Parker?"

Ah! It was them, wasn't it? She knew it. She could feel it in her gut.

"This is she."

"Hi, this is Shyanne from Great Listicles. I wanted to talk to you about the possibility of you becoming one of our verified contributors."

"Yes! I see that you are on top of your emails. I answered that barely three minutes ago."

"Oh yes. It's not every day we ask someone to join our team. I noticed that you actually haven't been a part of our site for very long, so it's pretty amazing to see that you've already reached this level of success in such a short amount of time."

"To be honest, I've been surprised by it myself. I just wrote about things I knew about, and people seem to like it."

"Well, it's your tone. You have an informal, sort of almost-sarcastic way to introduce topics, but then when you explain the positive reasons why, they sound quite genuine. Readers notice that kind of thing."

"Oh, well thank you. I appreciate that insight."

"Of course. That's what we're here for."

She went on, explaining the position and what was expected of it. She would need to continue to write an average of at least one article a day per week, and no more than three. It would certainly cut down on her output, but apparently it was so they didn't spam their followers or overwhelm them with featured articles by verified contributors. But the tradeoff was that she was paid a base amount every week as long as she hit a minimum, then she'd also receive better bonus milestones based on her click rate.

If she did all right, she would still be making more than she did in her best week on the site. And if she did great... well goodness, that would really be lovely, wouldn't it?

In the end, their conversation lasted a good hour before it wrapped up and Chastity could happily accept the position. Her mother had come to fetch her, and Keiko had come to lock up, so both of them ended up standing at the door, watching her curiously as she paced and talked.

Fortunately for her, they seemed to know that something important was happening, because they didn't interrupt at all until she finally hung up and placed the phone on the desk.

"What was that all about?" her mother asked, looking like she was almost afraid to know. Chastity couldn't blame her for that. A lot of the surprises in their lives recently had been pretty terrible.

"I got a job!" she cried, laughing like an absolute madwoman. "And I don't have to work nearly as hard as I've been doing. I probably won't even have to fill out any more surveys once I get started."

"Oh honey, that's wonderful! Let's go home and make something to celebrate. I think we have enough for a truly hearty meal."

"That sounds perfect," Chastity said, beaming at her. "Looks like we'll be able to hit the town a bit sooner than I thought, Keiko."

"I look forward to it. And congratulations, of course."

"Thanks. The timing is a bit uncanny, isn't it?"

There was the slightest hint of a smirk to her smile as she answered. "The Lord works in mysterious ways."

"You betcha."

They laughed, and the Parkers headed out while Keiko locked up the spare office and returned to her work. Chastity was on cloud nine the entire way back home, practically floating.

Finally, it was like the skies were parting and there was a little bit of sun after so much doom and gloom. She couldn't believe it, but at the same time, she was immensely relieved.

They arrived home in good time, having laughed and giggled the entire way back. Chastity wondered if she could keep this good mood forever and never have to succumb to her normal pessimistic overthinking. Probably not, but that didn't mean that she couldn't cherish it while it was available.

Their mailbox was practically full as they walked up, and Chastity let go of her mother's arms to grab it all. Heading in, she sorted the piles into bills, bills, more bills, and then medical stuff and junk mail.

But this time, she wasn't feeling overwhelmed as she stacked the envelopes. It would still take a bit to get on her feet —even if she started the full-time position right away. But she could do it. And she would be able to do it in time to keep them in the house.

The good thing, however, was that now that she knew she would at least have a baseline to go off of, she could work out some semblance of a budget. Grabbing the top of the pile, she opened it up while pulling her calendar towards her.

Looked like it was water first. Not a bad bill, and one that they were only a month behind on. But as she unfolded it and looked at the minimum due, she was surprised to see... nothing.

Wait.

What?

She looked down the letter expecting to see past due reminders and a two-month past due bill, but instead there was nothing except the month of the bill and the amount listed as zero. "That's impossible," she whispered to herself.

While that would have been nice, Chastity knew that now more than ever she needed the account balances to be correct. The last thing she wanted was to be presented with an even larger bill and more late penalties next month.

She felt a smile cross her face. Just thinking how wonderful it would be if this were true. She pictured a large red stamp mark, angled across the bottom of the page reading "PAID IN FULL."

Her smile faded as quickly as it had appeared as reality returned. The past few years she had learned not to expect things to turn out good just because it appeared that they would. How many times had she and her friends celebrated a new job, a new part, a chance to be the first ones cast in a new show? She could still hear her agent's words over the phone saying the contracts were being drawn up as they spoke. How many times had she woken up the next day to the reality that the movers and shakers in New York's entertainment world could and did make last minute changes? Or maybe, she wondered many times, if she'd been given the right information at all. There never seemed to be a process that controlled these decisions but rather who was making the decision. And the who appeared to change on a weekly basis.

One thing she did learn was that until you sign your name at the bottom of the page, there was no reason to celebrate. The last few years she had held to that way of thinking, and while she had been working somewhat steady, there had not been the breakthrough she had been striving for. She still felt the pull of the audience and she still felt the thrill of taking someone's words and turning them into a walking talking piece of art. Just thinking about it now sent chill bumps up and down her arms. She would get there, she knew she would, but right now she was exactly where she needed to be.

Looking back at the bill, she remembered that the amount had been somewhere around ninety dollars and that was with two late fees.

She turned the bill over and found the customer service number. After calling the number, the recording gave her several options. She chose option number three for all bill inquiries. As it rang, she took a deep breath.

"Thank you for calling, this is Karen, how may I help you today?" the lady asked like she had said it hundreds of times today already.

"Yes ma'am. I received my bill today and am pretty sure the balance is not correct. Could you check that for me?"

Chastity could hear tapping on a keyboard as they spoke.

"Yes ma'am. What is your name and account number?"

Chastity recited it to her just as it was written on the bill. "This is actually my mother's account. My father passed away recently, and I am helping her with her bills until we can get them all current and back on schedule."

The customer service representative didn't say anything in response to this information. Chastity suddenly felt very alone in dealing with these issues.

"There isn't a balance on the account. It's all paid off," she said, as if she was giving her good news.

"But that can't be right," Chasity said, raising her voice. She caught herself quickly and took a deep breath. "I haven't paid the amount due, and I need to get the correct balance."

The customer service rep was silent for a moment, as if wondering what to say. "Let me see if I can find out how this was paid," she said. "Are you listed on the account as well?"

"No," Chastity answered. "But my mom has given me power of attorney to handle all of her finances. I am really trying to get them straight."

The rep got quiet, then said, "Ms. Parker can you hold one moment? I need to get an access code from my supervisor to get into the payment part of the account."

"Yes ma'am, anything you can do to help me I would really appreciate," Chastity said, feeling hopeful that she might get some answers.

After a few minutes she came back on the phone. "Do you have the password for this account?"

Chastity quickly picked up a notebook where she had been jotting down as much information as she could find about each account. It had not been easy since her mother had not handled any of the bills. Now that her dad was gone, getting answers to simple questions had become a chore that required detective work. And she'd become painfully aware how bad off they were financially.

She gave the password to the customer service rep.

There was a long pause as she checked the account. Chastity started pacing back and forth now as she held the line. She began to think how she really needed to stay on top of these bills if she was ever going to get them paid down. It was so easy to assume that the companies didn't make mistakes, just the customers. She would never have thought to question the bill before this.

"I am looking at the payment history now, and it appears last week someone came to the main office and paid the bill in full. In the notes it states the payment was made in cash and a receipt was given to the person who paid."

Chastity froze. She didn't know what to say. She couldn't get her words out, and she didn't want the rep to hang up.

"But this is crazy. How can that be?" she finally said. She still didn't think it was correct. She took a deep breath to calm herself and her head begin to clear. "If someone other than my mother or I came in to access the account, wouldn't they need to provide you with an account number or a password?"

"No Ma'am. If someone is making a payment, it's not required. It would be required if someone wanted to get personal information about the account but not to make a payment. I am looking through the notes and I don't see any information other than the account was paid in full with cash. The person who paid was given a receipt. It does have the person's name who took the payment; would you like to speak to her?"

"Yes, please," Chastity said quickly.

"Hold one moment and I will transfer you. If you need anything else just let us know," she said sweetly. Chasity thanked her and the phone call was forwarded. After several rings, a woman's voice mail recording came on, stating that she was either on her phone or out of the office but if you would leave a message, she would be glad to return the call at her earliest convenience. Chastity waited for the beep but changed her mind about leaving a message. How was she going to explain to a perfect stranger that someone had paid her bill and she wanted, what? A physical description of the person who paid it? His name? She went blank on how to ask this question, so she just hung up.

She stared at her table, feeling overwhelmed again. Someone had paid off their entire bill. She couldn't believe it.

Part of her hoped it was exactly who she thought it was, but that was impossible. A week had gone by since their fight, and they hadn't said a word to each other since then. There was no way Ben would be off paying her bills when they were still fighting.

...right?

It had to be another family friend. Or perhaps the church. Maybe even Keiko. Their water bill was less than a hundred dollars after all, and she knew several people who could afford that.

But still...

Shaking, her hand went to the next bill, for their gas. That one was a pretty penny, sitting at a thousand dollars and that was after her making payments of ten dollars over the minimum since she had arrived. They were refusing to deliver any more gas until they had it below five hundred dollars, which meant winter was going to be hit hard if she didn't catch up in time.

Now that she was going to have a regular job, she knew she could do it, and yet she still wondered what was waiting for her in the envelope.

She opened it, her heart thundering. Zero due. Paid in full.

No. It wasn't possible.

This time her hands shot toward the next envelope. Electric. And the next envelope. Mortgage. And the next. Credit card.

Over and over again until she was surrounded by torn envelopes and rumpled letters, all of them saying the same thing.

Zero balance. Paid in full.

Tears were in Chastity's eyes as she tried to understand it. A hundred and fifty thousand dollars in debt, all gone. The mortgage was not only brought current, but it was paid off. Suddenly, the heavy burden that had been weighing down her soul was gone, leaving her completely untethered.

There was only one person she knew who could ever do something like this, and her heart quickly swelled in her chest.

Even when they were angry with each other.

Even when he thought that she didn't care about him.

Ben was still looking out for her.

She put her head in her hands and cried. For once they weren't unhappy tears, but they certainly were flavored with relief and other overwhelming emotions. She couldn't believe it. There really was no stop to his kindness.

"Mom!" she called, her mother having wandered upstairs to change into her lounging clothes while Chastity took care of the mail.

"Yes, dear?" her mom asked, peeking around the corner of the hall and down the stairs.

"I need to go out. Do you mind staying put for about an hour?"

"I think I could do that. Honestly, I was thinking of having a nap."

"Perfect. And you'll call me if you need anything, right?"

"Of course, dear. Go do what you have to do."

That was all Chastity needed. She bolted out the door, crying, laughing, and feeling freer than she had in ages.

The world was shifting for her again, everything changing and moving, but for once she welcomed it with open arms. She was a career woman now, who was going to be able to pay the bills solely off of what she created with her mind and her hands. It was insane that it took that for her to realize that she didn't need to prove to anyone that she was more than what they thought she could be.

Because she finally believed it herself.

And she had one other person to tell about the good news.

26

Ben

*B*en sprawled out across his bed, the thick comforter feeling good against his sore back. He hadn't been able to sleep well the past couple of days, so he had woken up around four in the morning to get even more work done on the barn they were renovating before Benji took care of the general chores for the day.

In reality, none of the brothers had to do the work around the barn because the workers were capable of handling it themselves, but he and most of the others liked being more hands-on. After all, it was the *Miller* Ranch, not the Long-term Family Friends Ranch. That would certainly be a mouthful.

Ugh.

It was into the afternoon, and Ben was trying to rouse himself to go work on the barn again now that the hottest part of the day had passed. But something was keeping him in his bed. He couldn't stop staring up at the ceiling; it was like he could see his future played against it as if it were a projection screen.

Except it really was more like daydreaming. So many futures, so few of them possible. He wondered if Chastity even knew what he did, and if she would resent him for it. But with all the bills paid, it gave her the option to leave whenever she wanted. She would no longer be held down by all the bills that had been drowning her.

She would have a choice.

And that gave him some peace. If she hightailed it, then maybe he would finally be able to let her go. And if she stayed... well, he had no idea what would happen then. He didn't really believe that she would.

That light in his room flickered, which meant someone was at the door. Considering that Ma was out in the coop again, and Pa was out teaching some of the next generation of workers some of the ins and outs of the ranch, he had no idea who it could be. His brothers would just text him.

So, who was it?

He didn't know, and his natural curiosity wouldn't let him ignore it. Begrudgingly, he got up and made the small trek down the hall.

He opened the door, still half in his thoughts, only to see a breathless, red-faced Chastity standing there.

"What are you—"

She didn't let him answer, instead flinging herself into his arms and crashing her mouth to his. He was shocked but welcomed the kiss with a flood of relief through his system.

All the uncertainty, all the doubt he'd had over the past week and a half, was gone. Evaporated by the feeling of her against him.

But eventually the more practical side of his brain kicked in and he pulled away gently, his large hands still lingering on her soft hips. As much as he wanted to give into his temptation and never come up for air, there were things they needed to talk about.

Sometimes he hated being practical.

"I didn't expect you here," he said, looking down at her and drinking in all of her expression.

Her eyes were red and puffy while her cheeks were wet. She had been crying.

"This morning, I certainly didn't expect to be *here*."

He wiped her sweat-beaded forehead with his sleeve before his thumbs whisked away the dampness on her cheeks.

"Then why are you here?"

"I know what you did."

The corner of his lip dragged up ever so slightly while his blood rushed through his veins. "That sounds like something out of a horror movie."

"But really, it's anything but, isn't it?" She looked behind him, her expression flickering a bit. He realized that she'd never seen his new attachment. Back when they were together, he had a room in the main house. "Could we have a seat?"

"Uh, yeah. I've got a sitting room. This way."

He was loath to let her go, but he pulled his hands away from her and turned.

A million thoughts were rushing through his head, as he was wondering what she was going to say or what she wanted. She seemed happy enough with his decision judging by the kiss. But just because she appreciated what he did didn't mean that she was going to stay.

And that was all right.

He didn't pay for everything in some ploy to buy her like a

common horse. No, he paid for those things for two reasons. One, was as an apology, but secondly was so that she could be free to make decisions that truly felt right to her. No worrying about money, or her mother depending on her. For once, she could think of only herself.

They reached his sitting room, a small place but with a loveseat and a comfortable recliner, a fireplace, and a bookshelf. He didn't use it often, considering that he lived alone, but every now and then he liked to sit with a good book and listen to the fire crackle while night fell outside of his bay window.

Chastity perched herself on the loveseat, curling her legs under her, and he took that as a good sign. She was settling in for at least a few minutes, not poised and ready to run.

"So..." he began slowly.

"So," she echoed.

Then it was quiet, neither of them knowing where to start. He felt like perhaps it was time for him to be quiet and listen to her, but she didn't seem to be ready to speak.

And so, he waited.

And waited.

But eventually, she did take a deep breath and started speaking.

"I got a job!"

Oh. That wasn't what he expected. "That's great! I didn't know you were looking for one."

"I was in a mad dash to try to get money to dig my parents out of their debt. But now," she paused, and there was so much emotion in her eyes that he felt his own heart squeeze.

He wished she had told him sooner, so she wouldn't have had to struggle so much, but he supposed that he hadn't earned her trust then.

"Now I don't have to worry about that, do I?"

Ben raised his eyebrows, trying to keep his expression neutral. "Whatever do you mean?"

But she smiled softly, her eyes welling up again. "Why did you do it, Ben?"

That tone. It wasn't condemning. It wasn't upset. But it was truly bewildered. He supposed that Chastity hadn't exactly had nice gestures thrown at her throughout her entire life.

"I did it for you."

Her head tilted ever so slightly to the side as she studied him. "To bribe me to stay here?"

"No, nothing like that." It seemed that it was time to use his words. It all seemed so overdramatic, like a real production, but he needed to express what was going on in his brain. *Chastity* needed to know what was going on in his brain.

"I did it because it feels like you have all these chains telling you what to do and how to live. Whether it's your responsibility you feel toward your mother, whether it's the expectations that were leveled against you as you grew up. Whether it was bills, or the bank man, or any number of things. It seemed that you couldn't make a choice solely for you, and that I would never be able to know how you truly felt.

"So, while I couldn't do anything about the expectations, or your relationship with your mother, I could take care of the rest, which would maybe give you enough room to figure the other things out on your own.

"And maybe, when all of that is said and done, I might be enough for you. And maybe I won't. But the important thing is that I would know that your decision came from you and no one else.

"And that's what I needed, and why I did it."

"Oh..." Her voice was quiet as she seemed to take in everything that he was saying. Silence won out again as she sat there, and he could practically see her mind doing flips.

"You wanted me to be free," she said finally, her eyes flitting to him.

Relief washed over Ben. She understood, and she didn't seem upset. So, while maybe she would thank him and then choose to leave forever, at least he knew that he had done the right thing.

But he desperately, intensely wished that she would stay. That she would stop letting those doubtful, cruel voices of the past dictate her life and instead, live true to her own self.

"I did."

She got up, and for a moment, he thought that this was goodbye, that she was going to walk out of the door grateful, but on her own path. Instead of leaving, however, she walked over to him and sank onto his lap, her back resting against one arm of the recliner and her legs draping over the other side.

"That new job I was telling you about? It's as a verified writer for this really popular site. Given that I don't have a literal mountain of debt crushing my mother or me anymore, in a month or two I should be able to get my own place in town. There's this cute little apartment I noticed on the way to the library. It's month-to-month, so I wouldn't be tethered down, but I think it might be worth staying in town for a bit."

It took everything inside of Ben for him not to jump to his feet and let out a triumphant yelp. Instead, he swallowed several times before he answered.

"Oh really?"

She nodded. "I'm not saying I'm giving up on my dreams of making it in the big city, but I think—for the moment—that I have everything I need. No matter what anybody says about me, I have a career now as a writer for an insanely popular website that literally thousands of people apply to every year. I didn't even apply! I was chosen.

"And..." her tone softened, and he could feel her face warm from where it was resting against his shoulder. "I don't want to be that far away from someone who cares so much about me that they would give anything to make sure I am happy.

"We have some things we need to work on, mostly with communication and listening, but I got your message loud and clear, Ben. I don't think I can ever forget it.

"So, if you're willing, I'd like to try this whole being together thing again. But as adults, which means no more grandiose promises we don't intend to fulfill, no more thinking the other should read our mind, no more bottling things up until they explode. We'll be open and honest about how we're feeling."

"And what if you go back to the city?"

"Well, we can try long distance. Or we can breakup. But that is a decision we would have to come to together. I won't lie to you; I still don't know where my life is headed, and I'm really excited about all the possibilities of this writing thing, but when I daydream about my future, it's better when you're involved."

"I think I can understand that." Ben shifted slightly, just enough to allow him to gaze at her face. "Chastity Parker, if you'd be so inclined, I'd like to court you."

Now she blushed scarlet and giggled ever so slightly. "I do declare, Mr. Miller, I think I might be inclined to say yes." She spoke with an overly exaggerated Southern accent, but he didn't care. She said yes—and that was all that mattered.

She said *yes*.

He couldn't hold back anymore, he leaned forward, his lips catching hers in an intense kiss. He felt her gasp, but she soon melted into him, and the passion consumed them both.

After so many years of longing, a decade of denying what he

wanted and everything he needed, after all those times saying he wasn't interested in romance, he finally had what his heart had been crying out for.

True, she had her flaws, but so did he. He lost his temper, and perhaps he had been a little too willing to blame her for everything. But that didn't matter now. The only thing that mattered was that they loved each other and were finally going to try again with all the trust they had refused to give each other before.

Eventually they parted, and he could hear both of them panting. His blood was rushing in his ears while the rest of his body was reacting viscerally to her presence. He wanted her; he wanted her more than anything.

Forcing himself to take a deep breath, he shifted slightly again. "Perhaps we should go on a walk? There's probably more things we should talk about."

Chastity looked like she wanted to say no, her lips slightly swollen from the need of their kiss and her face flushed, but after a beat she nodded and slid off of his lap. Offering Ben her hand once she was upright, she sent him a beaming grin.

"I don't think I've said it since I came back, but I love you, Ben. And I'm realizing I always have."

He stood and pulled her into another hug, his body singing as they touched once again. "And I love you, Chastity. But this time, I'm actually going to show it."

"Me too."

As tempting as it was to go right back to kissing in the chair —the two strolled out together.

And hopefully, together was how they would stay.

EPILOGUE

Chastity

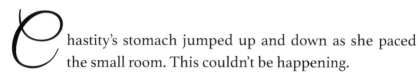hastity's stomach jumped up and down as she paced the small room. This couldn't be happening.

Was it really happening?

It was definitely happening.

Her teeth went to her nicely manicured fingernails again, biting down on her nail before the bitter taste of the polish reminded her to stop.

"Relax," Keiko said, gently running a hand over her arm. "Everything is going to go perfectly. You have nothing to worry about."

"Easy for you to say," Chastity said, not stopping her relentless march. "You're not the one getting married."

"Not yet," Mrs. Miller said, as she opened the door, giving the slender woman a wink.

But Keiko ignored that beyond her cheeks flushing slightly pink. She always had a knack for staying so poised.

"Take a deep breath, Chastity. This is what you've been waiting for ever since he proposed. You planned this whole thing. It's going to be perfect." Keiko adjusted her maid-of-honor dress.

"I know *it's* going to be perfect," Chastity said, flinging herself backward onto the bed, not caring if she rumpled her freshly done hair. "I'm worried about *me*."

"What do you mean?"

"Well, look at me! I'm Chastity. The fat, nerdy girl from high school, who excelled at drama club and almost nothing else. I went to New York City and totally failed after a decade of trying to make it big and had to come home with my tail between my legs."

"Is that how you see it?" Keiko asked. "Because what I see is an amazing woman who's made a career out of writing fascinating travel articles and became an online travel personality. People pay you to take amazing trips across the world and thousands of people look up to you.

"I see a woman who has an entire team of writers working under her that she handpicked from town. People who now have their comfortable livelihood thanks to you.

"I see a woman who never gives up. A woman who's always patient. A woman who walked her mother through one of the worst illnesses that you can have and came out the other side all the better for it.

"I'm not quite sure what you see, but I see a bride that any man would be incredibly lucky to have. And I think Ben would agree with me."

Chastity sat up and gave her best friend an earnest smile.

"You really do have a way with words, Keiko. You know it's not too late to join my team."

"I belong with the church. Although I don't mind guest posting every now and then." She offered her hand, and Chastity took it, allowing herself to be pulled to her feet. "Now, how about we get you dressed?"

Chastity nodded shakily, and both she and Mrs. Miller went about getting the dress out from where it had been hidden in the closet.

It had been a very intense two years since Chastity and Ben had decided to give their relationship a real try, and her life had changed entirely.

Starting with her mother. Finally, after what seemed like forever, the doctor was able to identify the type of dementia she had, and it was one that was relatively reversible. However, there was a lot of repair to be done, as he figured that she had been sick with it for over a year and that there had been a lot of internal damage to her brain from the stress.

So, she was on the appropriate meds now, and she had several rehabilitative nurses who came in twice a week to work with her, and a night nurse for as soon as the sun went down. Now that Chastity was on the Listicles' health insurance plan, she was able to take on her mother as a dependent and get her some better—and less expensive—medical care.

While she wasn't entirely back to normal, her mom's episodes were few and far between, and she seemed to have come to terms with her husband's death. Of course, there were bad days, but she knew she was only a call or a walk away from Chastity's place.

Naturally, things were going to be strange for a while as Chastity, her mom, and Ben moved into the house Ben and his brothers were building for them. Although she had her own place and Ben had his bachelor's attachment, neither of those places were really fit for the three of them to live together, and if Chastity was going to live on the ranch, she wanted to bring her mother with her.

She shuddered at the thought of them being an hour walk apart. Funny how she had lived an entire decade without much contact with her mother, and now they were practically inseparable.

"Arms up!"

She did so and soon the dress was being put over her head. For a moment, the world was just tulle, chiffon, and satin, but then the dress was on her body and being pulled into place by the two women.

It was a beautiful, white mermaid dress with an explosion of beautiful cloth just below her knees. It was made from a mix of both Mrs. Miller and her mother's dresses, the former happy to give up some of her own wedding dress because she didn't have any daughters of her own.

The dress made her feel like a princess from some fairytale kingdom—and she loved it.

Almost as much as she loved Ben.

Finally, the dress was fully on, and they were lacing her up. This was it. In just a short while, she would be Mrs. Benedict Miller. Crazy to believe that she had come here for her father's funeral and was ending up married to one of the most sought-after and richest bachelors in the whole area.

Not that the money mattered to her. She was loath to the idea of ever being a gold digger and had managed to amass a modest amount of wealth herself. She was by no means rich, but she and her mother were more comfortable than they had ever been.

Speaking of her mother, the door opened and her mother

quickly popped in, an expensive looking box in her hands. "I have the veil," she announced, rushing over. "I have the—"

She stopped short upon seeing Chastity, and her eyes instantly started to water. "Oh, my little girl..." she whispered, nearly dropping the veil.

Who could keep a straight face in front of such emotion? Chastity felt herself blush, and her own eyes watered.

"Hi, Mom," she said, her voice catching with emotion.

Her mom set the veil down and walked toward Chastity, enveloping her in a hug that was surprisingly tight.

"You look so beautiful," she said.

"I *feel* beautiful, Mom."

"I'm sorry your father isn't here to see you. He was always so proud of you."

Chastity's eyebrows raised. "Mom, we both know Dad didn't approve of any of my choices."

"Oh, honey. He loved you so much." Her mom looked into Chastity's eyes. "As your daddy, his number one priority was for his little girl to be safe. He worried about you. He wanted you to have a happy life and couldn't stand the thought of you getting hurt or being sad. When you were far away, he missed you being close."

"I never thought of it like that. So he was proud of me?"

"Yes, he was. I'm sorry you didn't know that," her mom said.

They held each other until there was a knocking of three short raps on the door. That was her signal.

The wedding had started.

Chastity and her mother parted, but their arms stayed linked around each other. Since Charles Parker had passed, it would be her mother who was giving her away.

"Are you ready?" Mrs. Miller asked, patting her cheek ever so lightly.

Chastity nodded, afraid that if she spoke she would break down into happy and nervous tears all over again.

"All right. I'll see you then. And if you make a break for it, remember the horses are to the south, not the west."

She laughed slightly, remembering that since they were being married in the gussied up main barn that all of the horses had been moved into the other barn that Ben and his brothers had finished renovating before the last winter.

"Good to know."

Mrs. Miller nodded then headed out the door, no doubt to walk down the aisle with her son to sit at the first seat on his side.

"Time for me to go too," Keiko said. She adjusted Chastity's veil to be perfect, gave her a warm hug, and went to take her place at the front of the church.

She had a rather small number of attendants. And by small, it was just Keiko, who was her maid-of-honor. One of Ben's cousin's children was the flower girl, and they had decided to forgo a ring bearer entirely.

Of course, his party was much fuller, with all of his brothers agreeing to see the eldest marry—even Bryant, who promised to be on his best behavior. That boy had really turned things around in the past year, but that was a story for another day.

"Ready?" her mother asked, looking up at her with loving eyes.

"Ready," Chastity said, her emotions already threatening to overwhelm her.

But it was a good sort of overwhelmed. One that filled her with happiness from her toes all the way up to her scalp. She was so stuffed full of joy that she wouldn't be surprised if she glowed in the dark.

Life seemed to become a bit surreal as she left the building that was Ben's bachelor attachment. It would soon be someone else's, as Ben wouldn't be needing it anymore. Likely, none of the brothers would move into it, considering they all had their own places. But she was sure the Millers would find some way to make it of use.

It was a short walk to the main barn. Ben's brother Benji had spent the last few days building a beautiful, lacy canopy to walk under. Chastity didn't even want to think of how much money the Miller family had spent on her nuptials, but Mrs. Miller had insisted on being in charge of the finances and wouldn't let her look at any of the receipts. Normally, Chastity would never allow someone to override her on something so important, but considering she was the first Miller marriage of the current generation, she didn't see what was wrong with letting the matriarch do what she willed.

"Here we are," her mother said.

The barn loomed in her vision, and they were only a few feet from the open barn doors. Her senses awakened as she inhaled a lovely pine scent mixed with wood and fresh hay. She heard the processional music start, and the moment she had dreamed of but never thought would be real had arrived. Generations of Millers had married and started families here. And Chastity realized with a tug at her heart that this was something to cherish, not to run away from. Maybe this beautiful feeling of belonging is what her father and mother had wished for her all these years.

The light dimmed as she passed through the large door, with the candles flickering against the barn walls creating a soft glow. Everyone stood to see her. Her stomach lurched again, but all of that nervousness came to a grinding halt as her eyes landed on Ben.

Oh goodness.

He stood there, tall and illuminated by the sunlight streaming in through one of the windows, looking like a handsome statue in his clean, pressed suit.

Their wedding colors were black, white, and blue, and those fit him perfectly. His tux was black, but his vest was blue, which made his green eyes shine that much brighter. But it wasn't his looks that captured her, rather the expression in his gaze as their eyes met.

How could he fit so many words into a single look? Love, attraction, relief, amazement. All of them swirled within his green orbs and left her utterly speechless.

"Oh dear," she whispered as she felt the tears come on. Thank goodness Keiko had insisted that she only use waterproof mascara and eye makeup for her big day.

"You all right?" her mother whispered.

"I'm more than all right," Chastity answered, her voice warbling from the tears. "I think I'm as happy as is possible for a single human to be right now."

"Good. This feeling will last for the rest of your life if you do it right. Your father and I always wanted you to experience a relationship full of love like we shared. There's nothing better."

Chastity squeezed her mom's arm tight, as the realization of how much her parents loved her and wanted the best for her caused a lump in her throat.

Her dress swished and rustled on the aisle runner that created a path for her on the hay. A path to her future. They reached the end of the aisle, and then the reverend was asking who was giving her away. Her mother answered, and the next thing that Chastity knew, she was walking up to face Ben.

The world fell away, and it was just the two of them, existing in their own bubble of love. The reverend kept talking, saying all the things that he was supposed to, but she didn't pay much attention until it was time for their vows.

She went first, and every word was a struggle. She wanted to throw her arms around Ben and never stop kissing him, but she managed to contain herself for a bit longer.

"I, Chastity Parker, promise to love and cherish you, Benedict Miller, as much as you have loved and cherished me in these past years together. I promise to always include you in my dreams, no matter how grandiose and faraway they are.

"You are my first thought in my morning, and my last thought at night. I will hold you close to my heart, and make sure your home will always be there."

By the end she was a sobbing mess, and Ben wasn't doing much better. Granted, he had a much classier cry than her.

"I, Benedict Miller, promise you, Chastity Parker, that I will love you until the end of time. I promise to never clip your wings or stand in the way of any of your dreams. I will always support you, always believe in you, and although I may not understand your next great scheme, I'll follow you through it to the other side of the world and back.

"I know it's cliché to say that you are my light, but you are. You are the sun that greets me every morning, and my hope for a grand future. You give me reason to be, and I promise to never forget that. I love you, Chastity, and I can't imagine ever living without you."

He leaned forward to kiss her, but the reverend cleared his throat and stopped him at the last moment.

Right.

There were still more words to go before the kissing could take place. But it was hard to wait.

A few light chuckles filtered through the wedding, and

Chastity felt her cheeks redden, but it gave them both a chance to collect themselves before the holy man continued.

"Do you, Benedict Miller, take this woman to be your lawfully wedded wife? To have and to hold, in sickness and in health, for better or for worse?"

"I do," he whispered, his green eyes still staring into hers.

"And do you, Chastity Parker, take this man to be your husband? To have and to hold, for better or for worse, and in sickness and in health?"

"I do."

They had decided to leave out the part about if anyone objected. Because if they did, but they hadn't expressed it so far, they certainly weren't welcome at the wedding.

"Then you may kiss the bride."

And boy did he.

They reached for each other like opposite ends of a magnet, their lips colliding in the perfect kiss. Chastity couldn't tell anyone how long they stayed in each other's embrace, but when they finally broke apart, the entire barn cheered.

They had done it! They had really done it!

After a whole lot of struggle, and several very large mishaps, they were finally married.

It was time to begin their happily ever after.

Starting with their wedding night.

BEN CARRIED Chastity across the threshold into the honeymoon suite at the Caribbean resort. He placed her on the bed on the cushy comforter that felt like a pillow for her whole body.

"You look beautiful like that," Ben said.

"I look beautiful with unbrushed hair, still wearing yesterday's makeup and suffering from jet lag?"

"All I see is my new wife on our bed." Ben leaned over to kiss her forehead.

Chastity let out a contented sigh.

He winked. "Are you tired? Maybe we should just rest. We've certainly had a long weekend."

"No!" Chastity declared, sitting up. "I've managed to keep my hands to only the appropriate places for two years. I've been planning this ever since you proposed, and I won't let some pesky jet lag ruin it."

"Really, ever since I proposed? I feel a bit objectified now."

She gave him a look. "Are you trying to pretend that you didn't feel the same?"

"I guess you may have a point. Except for me it's been since high school."

Chastity's eyes opened wide and her eyebrows raised. With a shot of adrenaline, she rolled off the bed and stood up, her hands going to her hips, elbows jutting out. "Exactly! I need to go freshen up. Why don't you make yourself comfortable and unpack or something."

"Yes, princess." He winked again. "Your wish is my command."

"Shush you," Chastity said before grabbing her suitcase and wiggling her behind at him as she marched to the bathroom.

She rushed through washing her face and then filled the deep tub that looked so tempting. After pouring in a complimentary packet of rose oil, she stepped into the tub and shaved.

She had to admit that her stomach was doing flip-flops with nerves. After all these years, they didn't have to stop at just kissing. She couldn't believe this was all real, and yet here she was, on her honeymoon with a man who adored her.

The warm, scented water was pure heaven, relieving the strain from the wedding and the long flight. Her head lolled back, and finally, she let herself relax, trying to calm her nerves.

When the anticipation became too great, she let the water drain out of the tub as she dried off and rubbed a romantic, scented lotion on her body. Then she put on a beautiful piece of elegant lingerie that Keiko had given her as a wedding shower gift.

Chastity opened the bathroom door to see Ben pacing the floor. He turned to look at her, and his eyes grew wide. A huge smile appeared on his face.

"Hey there, my beautiful wife," Ben said, coming toward her and kissing her forehead.

With his strong hands, he gently caressed her neck and shoulders, kissing lightly on her soft skin.

"Mmm. You smell and taste delicious," he said.

"That feels wonderful," Chastity said, her nerves starting to melt. "Please don't stop."

He kissed her eyelids, cheeks, tip of her nose, then down her neck. His hands continued caressing as he took a step back to admire her body.

"You are even more perfect than I could have imagined," he said.

Chastity smiled, feeling adored and loved, as she stepped to Ben, put her arms around his neck, and kissed him on the lips.

Ben gave a low growl and wrapped his arms around her. They kissed passionately until he scooped her up in his arms. He set her on the bed and pressed a gentle kiss to her lips. Chastity pushed into it, heat building in her core.

She pulled him deeper into the embrace, hoping he could feel her desire, her love through every touch. He responded, and soon he was pressing into her with a sort of urgency that they had never allowed before.

His hands caressed over her, reverent, loving, touching her in all the ways a husband was supposed to touch. Her heart and her body sang out in happiness, finally having what they had both craved for so long.

She looked up into his eyes, taking in every feature of his face. She wanted to burn this moment into her memory for all of time.

They went slowly, carefully, both of them new to what they were doing. But they joined as only two souls in love could join, and Chastity swore she had never experienced such soaring bliss.

"I love you," tumbled from both of their lips, as they grew lost in each other.

She loved Ben with all her heart. She would never leave him again. It was almost impossible to believe that he was really there, but he was. He wasn't going anywhere, and for once, neither was she.

It was a happily ever after indeed.

DID you like reading about Chastity and Ben? Are you ready to read another, possibly even better story about Ben's brother Bart? Well, Brothers of Miller Ranch Book Two is ready for you to read! And the reviews are nothing short of amazing! Take a look for yourself and decide if you want to read it.

OR, go ahead and buy the whole box set at a great deal! There are over 300 STELLAR reviews combined on this series! I don't think you'll be disappointed! You can find my Brothers of Miller Ranch Box Set on Amazon.

AUTHOR'S NOTE

Hello Reader!

I'm so happy you've made it to this point in my very FIRST Contemporary Western Romance! I hope you loved getting to know the modern day Miller family. There are four more books in this series! Each book is about Ben's other brothers falling in love.

Also, since readers have enjoyed Brothers of Miller Ranch so much, I've started another series that's a spin-off of this series. PLUS, the first book of the new series is FREE! If you are a part of my newsletter, you should have already gotten it. If you haven't joined my newsletter yet you will get that free book once you join.

Find out more here: nataliedeanauthor.com

Also, if you're interested, I've got a short series available about the Miller's of the 1800s! It's called *Brides of Miller Ranch*. In that series, you'll read about Juniper (the Juniper that Juniper's Grove is named after), and two other amazing couples of the 1800s Miller Ranch. That's why you'll find stories from Ben and his brothers' ancestors of years ago intertwined throughout this modern take off of Miller Ranch.

You can only find the *Brides of Miller Ranch* historical series in my Brides & Twins Mail Order Bride Compilation. It is the second series within that set of books. If you like historical westerns, you'll love it!

EXCLUSIVE BOOKS BY NATALIE DEAN

GET THREE FREE BOOKS when you join my Sweet Romance Newsletter :)

Get One Free Contemporary Western Romance:
The New Cowboy at Miller Ranch - He's a rich Texas rancher. She's just a tomboy ranch employee. Can she make him see life can still be happy without all that money?

AND Two Free Historical Western Romances:
Spring Rose - A feel good historical western mail-order groom novelette about a broken widow finding love and faith.

Fools Rush In - A historical western mail-order bride novelette based off a true story!

Go to nataliedeanauthor.com to find out how to join!

IF YOU ENJOYED THIS STORY...

Please be so kind as to leave an honest review. Reviews can make or break the success of a book and help readers such as yourself decide whether or not they might want to read the book. Even if you only write a few words, it makes a big difference! Thank you so much...

LAWMEN'S BRIDES SERIES (Historical)

The Ranger's Wife

Benjamin's Bride

Carson's Christmas Bride

Justin's Captive Bride

BRIDES AND TWINS SERIES (Historical)

A Soldier's Love

Taming the Rancher

The Wrong Bride

A Surprise Love

The Last Sister's Love

BRIDES & TWINS Box Set / Mail-Order Bride Compilation (My best-seller! It includes TWO MORE unreleased heartwarming mail-order bride series)

LOVE ON THE TRAILS SERIES (Historical)

A Love Beyond Suspicion

Picture Perfect Love

Love of a Wild Rose

A Dangerous Time to Love

A Cold Winter's Love

Brides, Trails, and Mountain Men

Historical Western Romance Compilation

Includes my *Love on the Trails Series* plus an exclusive series titled *Marrying a Mountain Man*

BOULDER BRIDES SERIES (Historical)

The Teacher's Bride

The Independent Bride

The Perfect Bride

The Indian's Bride

The Civil War Bride

BOULDER BRIDES BOX SET

BRIDES OF BANNACK SERIES (Historical)

Lottie

Cecilia

Sarah

Though I try to keep this list updated in each book, you may also visit my website nataliedeanauthor.com for the most up to date information on my book list.

ABOUT AUTHOR - NATALIE DEAN

Born and raised in a small coastal town in the south I realized at a young age that I was more adventurous than my conservative friends and family. I loved to travel. My passion for travel opened up a whole new world and new cultures to me that I will always be grateful for.

I was raised to treasure family. I always knew that at some point in my life I would leave my storybook life behind and become someone's mother, someone's aunt and hopefully someone's grandmother. Little did I know that the birth of my son later in life would make me the happiest I've ever been. He will always be my biggest achievement. The strong desire to be a work-from-home mom is what lead me down this path of publishing books.

While I have always loved reading I never realized how much I would love writing until I started. I feel like each one of my books have been influenced by someone or something I've experienced in my life. To be able to share this gift has become a dream come true.

I hope you enjoy reading them as much as I have enjoyed creating them. I truly hope to develop an ongoing relationship with all of my readers that lasts into my last days :)

www.nataliedeanauthor.com

facebook.com/nataliedeanromance

Made in the USA
Monee, IL
15 September 2021